THE
TWINS

THE
TWINS

KELLY LYNN COLBY

Cursed Dragon Ship
PUBLISHING

Copyright © 2023 by Kelly Lynn Colby

Cursed Dragon Ship Publishing, LLC

6046 FM 2920 Rd, #231, Spring, TX 77379

captwyvern@curseddragonship.com

Cover © 2023 by Stefanie Saw

Developmental Edit by Kelly Lynn Colby

Proofread by S.G. George

ISBN 978-1-951445-51-5

ISBN 978-1-951445-50-8 (ebook)

This book is a work of fiction fresh from the author's imagination. Any resemblance to actual persons or places is mere coincidence.

This one's for my children who simultaneously keep me young and age me prematurely. I'm grateful you were not twins.

Chapter One

The deepening dark of the Fourth of July sky hung heavy with the smell of gunpowder. It had rained on and off for hours. So as soon as there was a break, though it wasn't quite night yet, many revelers lit a ton of fireworks. Not my younger brother, though. Bad weather or no, Sparrow wasn't about to start the show early. The rain would wait for him; he was sure of it. And I believed him.

I wasn't sure how I felt about the holiday, but this particular BBQ gave me the warm and fuzzies. Standing on the weed-free lawn under the row of precisely trimmed crepe myrtles, I was sure someone was set up taking pictures for the next cover of *Suburban Perfection,* a magazine I just made up that would star Sparrow and Tori and their angelic little boys.

Flores bumped my shoulder as he handed me a fresh margarita in a red, white, and blue plastic cup. "Fauna, your brother doesn't skimp on the tequila."

"He doesn't skimp on the decorations either." As I took a sip of the mixed drink, I couldn't help but admire the work they dedicated to the overall visual appeal of tonight's performance. American flags lined the driveway and sidewalk. The gas lamp was wrapped in red, white, and blue crepe paper. The pop-ups that protected the potluck dishes flashed with fans, swirls, pennants, fringe, pom poms, and balloons in the holiday colors. How had they managed to get this all done without a staff? My blue sequined shirt and bright red flip-flops were the extent of the Fourth of July decorations I owned.

With a huge plate—decorated with the Stars and Stripes, of course—full of smoked brisket, beans, and corn on the cob, Amelia handed me her drink to free up a hand. "Too bad Gina went home for the holiday. She'd love all the kids running around."

Things with Amelia and I were still a bit tense after I tried to sap energy from her while in my super high state after almost dying. Yet, she came anyway. I'd almost cried when her car pulled up. We'd fix it. Somehow.

A car turned down the street, just as my nephew, Cooper, headed toward the asphalt. Flores dived into action. But the neighborhood adults—and a few of the older children—yelled, "Car!" and Cooper froze still on the sidewalk. Anyone in the street scattered out of the way until the car drove by. Then the fun resumed like there hadn't been an interruption at all.

Flores wiped sweat from his brow. "Gina would *enjoy* this? I think I'm about to have a heart attack." I'd never seen him so on edge, not even at a murder scene.

Amelia lifted an eyebrow and a shoulder, her mouth too full to answer.

My scalp tickled with Flores's anxiety, but only barely. Public existence had become more and more bearable the more I practiced my new techniques. "I used to think the same thing. She's with fourth-graders all day. Why would she want to spend more time with kids? But she's just built for it or something. She loves it."

Finally swallowing, Amelia added, "If things progress with Daryl, I hope he's prepared for a whole gaggle at home."

Daryl was Gina's boyfriend she met volunteering at St. Benedict's. I'd never seen her so serious with anyone. Every time I saw them together, the air vibrated with love warming my entire body. "Wait. Is that why she went home to celebrate? She took Daryl with her, didn't she?" I felt so disconnected from my closest friends. I didn't like it.

Amelia nodded, the corn cob between her teeth shaking with her. "One of us has to have kids. We can't spoil just your brother's."

She had a point. Amelia and I had vowed to never reproduce. I wouldn't pass on this curse, and Amelia's parents did such a number on her, she didn't want history to repeat itself. It was the one girlfriend pact Gina wouldn't agree to. "True. We'll be the best aunties ever across a multitude of children." I turned to Flores. "What about you? Do you and Austin have any plans to expand your family?"

The tough-as-nails cop softened, and his cheeks flushed. "We've just been approved as a foster family."

Foster family? How had I missed that turn of events? Since I could sense the emotions of those around me, I was not frequently surprised by things.

Amelia took it in stride. "Sweet. We'll have all kinds of kids to shop for at Christmas time and never have to pay a dime of tuition."

While I digested this news, Austin came out of the house carrying a refreshed bowl of potato salad. Beside him, my sister-in-law, Tori, chatted animatedly with a pitcher full of liquid refreshment in each hand. Yet, somehow, she didn't spill a drop. I wasn't sure if I was supposed to worship her or hate her. She was everything I could never be, but domestic bliss wasn't exactly one of my life ambitions either. Sparrow was the only one of us siblings who'd managed to find some sort of normalcy.

Of course, he wasn't an empath.

Austin waved as best he could with his hands full of another Fourth of July–colored bowl. Did Tori own any regular dishware?

Flores lifted his cup to Amelia and me. "I better see to my husband before he redecorates Tori's interior."

As he jogged off, I tilted my head at Amelia. "Flores hasn't been inside, has he? That place could be featured on HGTV."

Warmth flowed through my skin, and I knew immediately who the source was. "Heidi, it's about time Forrest let you come say, 'Hi!'"

Since I couldn't feel him, I about dropped my drink when Forrest whispered, "Boo," in my ear.

With a gentle shove, I pushed my older brother back and leaned toward his girlfriend. "I see you haven't gotten rid of him yet. Don't forget our safe word: *willow wisp*. One alliteration later, and I'll have you safely away."

Heidi's smile was enough to light up a room, whether it was natural or because of her healing abilities, I would never know. Because of her gift, the scar tissue from my stabbing was no more than a distant memory. And she never punished me for doubting she could do it. The fact that I picked up the same skill was the real mystery. Empathy wasn't contagious—normally.

Heidi cheered with me. "Don't worry. I've got it covered." She raised her left hand where a simple, yet elegant diamond ring in white gold sparkled in the failing light.

Amelia choked on her corn, and I almost dropped both margaritas. "Holy shit, Forrest. I mean, it is Forrest, right?"

My older brother shook his head and simply smiled. Heidi wrapped herself around his left arm. "I know, it's shocking, but when he asked me, it felt inevitable. We make a great team."

Before I said something I would regret about how their teamwork made a bunch of people sick, Amelia nodded at Sparrow and Uncle Bertram who approached us. "Well, this seems like a family discussion. I'm going to see if I can find a sink, or maybe a hose, to get the delicious remnants off my face."

When Forrest wrapped his right arm around Sparrow's neck to ruffle his hair, Heidi slipped out from his grip. "Wait up, Amelia. I haven't had dessert yet. Let's divide and conquer."

"Yes!" Amelia pumped an elbow. "If we each fill a plate, we can try *everything*."

Now surrounded by my brothers and estranged uncle—wearing a dark colored newsboy cap like he was some sort of celebrity trying to escape the paparazzi—I tried to come up with an excuse to run away too. I mean, I liked dessert much more than I liked tense family discussions. Thankfully, Sparrow was better at starting them than I was.

"I'm so glad you all were able to make it." Sparrow held up his wooden mug with *Grill Master* carved into it. "To family."

"To family." We all repeated.

Though my toes and fingertips tickled with Sparrow's happiness, I couldn't mirror the same feeling. It had been months since the last awkward barbecue where we found out Bertram was moving into town and wanted to reignite our relationship. I hadn't seen him since, despite the multiple times he'd texted or sent me emails. The memory of Mom's fear whenever he was around was enough to cause my gut to tighten every time I saw him. The worst part was I had nothing to back up that instinctive reaction. Bertram had never done anything to harm us, though he didn't help one bit when we were homeless, running from shelter to shelter, motel to motel, either. And he could afford it.

Yet somehow, after abandoning his own brother's children, he'd chosen to adopt two unrelated orphans later in life. After taking a sip from both margaritas I held, maybe that was the safest topic to concentrate on. "How are Emblyn and Emmett adjusting to Houston?"

Bertram swelled with pride that warmed my body deeper than the humid summer air. "Those kids are tougher than most adults I know. But we won't truly know until they start school in the fall."

Sparrow's smile grew as he gestured toward his boys throwing snaps on the ground as the older kids rode their bikes through the made-up obstacles. "Cooper will show them around, and Justin will follow them like a lost puppy."

"I think they're happy to have other children to play with."

Bertram placed a fatherly hand on Sparrow's shoulder, and a spike of jealousy cut through the warmth in my gut.

I didn't want a relationship with Bertram. I had no reason to be jealous of his and Sparrow's closeness. But I did envy my brother's ability to let the past go and move on with his life. Of course, the past didn't literally haunt him if he touched the wrong object.

Bertram's face turned serious as he leaned toward Forrest. "I have been meaning to ask you if you sense anything from Emblyn or Emmett. Every now and again, there's something that seems off. They remind me of you two when you were their age."

Forrest could sense empathic abilities in others. Were their possible abilities why Bertram had adopted them? But I thought that was why he avoided Forrest and I, only really communicating with Sparrow over the years.

Sparrow looked uncomfortable for the first time. "They're just kids, Bertram." He knew damn well Forrest and I were different, but he liked to pretend he came from a perfectly normal family. I reconsidered the perfect suburban scene on the patriotic holiday. Maybe that was why he tried so hard to make everything look ideal. He was overcompensating.

At least he had some sanity left. Forrest and I were likely lost causes.

Bertram wasn't an empath. If he was, he would've stopped asking questions as the tension amped up around him. "I just need to know so I can protect them. I failed you three, and I don't want that to happen again."

I guzzled the rest of my margarita and took a hefty sip of Amelia's, refusing to look anyone in the eye.

"I did think I felt something, but it wavered and dissipated, which I've never experienced before. I'm not sure what it means." Forrest let out a deep breath. "Though between us, I've sensed many more empaths lately than ever. It's like there's more."

"Good, because there's something I've been meaning to tell you. Soon—"

Before Bertram could finish his sentence, a single firework shot from the back of Sparrow's truck in the driveway. Right behind it ran Emblyn, Emmett, Cooper, and Justin. Flores was closer to the truck than the rest of us and dropped a lit sparkler into his beer before it ignited the rest of the stash.

Set to explode himself, Sparrow clenched his fists. "Ever since Cooper learned how to start a fire in Cub Scouts, he's been lighting everything he can: candles, the stove, the fire pit out back, and now, apparently, fireworks." He threw his arms up in the air. "That's it. I'm going to track him down and take away that fire chit."

Flores offered his assistance. "Need help from a badge?"

"For Cooper, I'll take whatever assistance is offered." Sparrow nodded for Flores to follow him as Tori ran down from the porch to see what happened.

Bertram tilted his head at the twins who hid behind the neighbor's neatly trimmed English boxwoods. "Or maybe Cooper had nothing to do with this fire."

Forrest and I exchanged raised eyebrows.

Bertram dropped this hands into his pockets. "Well, since they're so eager to get started, I say let's indulge them. Fireworks time?"

Chapter Two

Too early on Friday, the parking lot at Chipped was empty. After the previous night's celebrations, I was certain few people were concerned with computer repairs. Though I suspected we'd get more than a couple coming in with phones that dropped in pools. One year, a dripping laptop came in. I wasn't sure what miracle they thought I could perform, but desperate people expect the extraordinary. Which was exactly what they thought I'd delivered after I'd manage to download most of their files from a cloud server they didn't even know they had set up. While that customer sang my praises for my genius, it was much easier to convince them to purchase one of the refurbed laptops.

When I walked into my little piece of independence, the sound of a vacuum greeted my ears. Now that I had a handful of corporate gigs to stabilize business, I needed another hand in the store to keep things running smoothly. Maggie had been the first one to apply, and I hired her immediately. She exuded confidence and curiosity, the two things necessary to start a new career, which was her intention. Plus, I felt for her and her foster care background. She had no one and I'd never forget what that felt like.

After only two weeks, I completely trusted her. "Hey, Maggie. It's looking good."

Though she was legally an adult, she still looked like a teenager with her bouncy walnut-colored hair and firm, sun-kissed skin. The sweet innocence in her eyes put me at ease. "Thank you, Ms. Fauna. Did you know that dust is mostly dead human skin cells? When I found that out, I couldn't tolerate a speck of it."

She did have a knack for talking too much, though. "Well, you've chosen the wrong business, then. Dust and computers go hand in hand. There's no avoiding it."

Maggie's face paled and her lips turned white. "Seriously?"

"Yep." I expected to feel innocent surprise or teasing amusement, but instead my stomach cramped from Maggie's fear. Maybe I shouldn't tease her so much. She was still getting used to life as an adult with zero support system to back her up. I related more than I'd like to admit. At least she wasn't out conning grieving people. She was one step ahead of me at that age. "But we have all kinds of vacuums to keep the dust at bay. And these awesome cans of air to clean out the keyboards." I pulled one out from under the counter and showed her how to use it on the register.

Her color returned to normal. Our hands brushed as she reached for the can. The back of my eyes burned, and I had to fight back tears. No matter what she was feeling, Maggie always had a deep sadness underneath it all. It took every fiber of my being to not snatch my hand back. Her gentle smile as she played with the compressed air made the effort worth it. Maybe I'd never have children, but at least I could help this young woman find her place. The last thing she needed was a sign of repulsion from me, even if she didn't understand where it came from.

"I'm going to head in the back and check on deliveries."

Maggie didn't look up from her newfound cleaning accessory. I rubbed my hands together to brush off the remaining sadness. Being able to function in my store without my gloves was an accomplishment on its own. I still felt everything but had it down to the numbing level without a single drop of alcohol. The Collective had helped me in immeasurable ways. I wished Mom could see me now. I wished Mom had found a group. Maybe she would have learned how to lessen her own torment and survive in this world just a bit longer.

Well, I guess I didn't rub all the sadness away. My phone buzzed with a text message.

Sparrow: Justin asked me to invite you to his soccer game tomorrow morning. Busy?

How sweet. But did I truly want to be surrounded by kids? They always seemed to carry one sickness or another with little glowy spots all over them. I had much better control over my emotionally empathy, but not the healing ability I picked up. One errand touch by a snotty nose and I'd be down for the rest of the day. Would it be weird to wear gloves and long sleeves to an outdoor soccer game in July in Houston?

Sparrow: Full disclosure. Bertram and the twins are coming as well.

Hm, I was curious about the Ems. If they were empaths, maybe I could help guide them early, before they became as fucked up as the rest of us. I must have waited too long to answer.

Sparrow: I know how you feel about crowds though, so I totally understand if you can't make it.

Me: Of course I'll come. Send me the address.

Sparrow: The boys will be thrilled. See you soon.

When my phone dinged with the address, I noticed I'd missed a call from Tucker. Things had been awkward between us since the Wasting Sickness incident. He was still confused by my sudden recovery and couldn't explain what had happened to him. I couldn't very well tell him that Heidi—and somehow me now —could heal people with our minds. The whole thing was ridiculous. How could a gorgeous, brilliant doctor believe any of this bullshit? He was the best thing that had ever happened to me romantically, yet I couldn't imagine how we'd have a future since I couldn't be completely honest about what I was.

My chest felt tight, but I was determined. I hit the button on Tucker's missed call and set it to speaker. Dropping the phone on my desk, I sat on my hands so I wouldn't change my mind and hang up.

His deep voice that both calmed my nerves and excited my senses greeted me. "Hey, Fauna. Thanks for calling me back."

Well, that was much more formal than I was expecting. It threw me off my focus. "Uh, you're welcome?"

He coughed. "I know you have that meeting tonight"—he didn't know what the meeting was about, and I found myself hopeful that everything was fine because he remembered it at all —"so can we have dinner Saturday night?"

My instinct was to say something dirty. That was always my mode of self-protection and that bit of me was on high alert. But his serious tone warned me not to be flippant. "Saturday night sounds great. Dress code?"

I couldn't feel his emotions over the phone, but his voice certainly sounded sad. "Nice, but not opera. I'll send you the address of the restaurant. See you soon."

He hung up before I could ask any further questions—or back out. When my phone binged with the second address, I realized how booked my open Saturday had just become. Luckily, Maggie and Jeff worked together incredibly well.

Before I asked her to fill in tomorrow, the back door chimed with a delivery. Time to make the donuts.

Chapter Three

The Tracy Gee Community Center glowed under the yellowed lights of the parking lot. This place hosted the group who saved my life—or at least made it a bit more bearable. I'd tried to convince them to take our weekly meetings to a bar, but the Collective voted to keep it at this modest, one-story building tucked in between much larger high rises. It was the last place they'd seen Debra alive, which somehow made it holy to them. I barely knew her, but still felt responsible for her death. Who was I to demand a move?

Inside, the mildew inherent to most buildings over a decade old in Houston mixed with stale perfume and old sweat from the yoga class. After months of entering these doors, the odor comforted me and programmed my brain like Pavlov's dogs to soften my stress and prepare to open up and hear and listen. Not sure I'd order a candle with that particular scent, but I appreciated the effect.

"Welcome, Fauna. We'll get started in a moment. Rodney's running late." Ademi greeted me with warmth but stern determination. She didn't like when things ran behind schedule. Her fabric design business likely ran like a well-oiled machine. That made me wonder if she needed technical support. I could add Ademi's World Designs to my roster.

After waving at Enrique, who leaned conspiratorially close to Margaret—whom he had giggling, probably with some dirty story—I moved toward Belinda at her normal spot, pacing by the window. She never spoke, but her face usually communicated anything we needed to know. I'd once asked why she was mute. Ademi explained that Belinda had been through serious trauma when she was young and hadn't uttered a word since. Apparently Belinda came from a wealthy family and even with the best tutors, she never managed to learn sign language. Whether from willful stubbornness or because it never clicked, no one knew. She could read and write just fine though, and used that skill whenever it became crucial for her to communicate a finer point. Nevertheless, Belinda chose to use her face to express her thoughts. Not that the people in this particular group needed the facial expressions to read her emotions.

While we awaited Rodney, it was a good time to ask Belinda for a favor. "Hey, girl."

Her feet slowed their movement, though she still bounced a bit in one spot. How much coffee had she drank? Belinda's genuine smile sent her happiness into my toes and fingers. Now that I had my empathy under control, the flow of others' emotions manifested as a minor memory of a feeling instead of an overwhelming tsunami of force. Most of the time, anyway.

"Can I ask a favor?"

She tilted her head, her graying hair slipping to one side of her face.

"Would you mind coming to a kids' soccer game with me tomorrow? My uncle's adopted twins might be empaths, and I was hoping for a second opinion."

Belinda clapped her hands together and offered a full-toothed grin.

"You do love discovering more people for our club, don't you?"

A sharp nod showed her agreement with my statement.

Rodney's anxiety pushed into the room ahead of him, making all of us turn before he'd entered. "Ha! I made it. Houston traffic will not thwart me."

Ademi's red-painted lips quirked up on one side as she took her seat—the cue for the rest of us to follow suit. Everyone except Belinda, of course. "So who has news to share?"

Enrique leaned against the back of his chair and crossed his legs. "I have a new boyfriend."

Belinda scoffed, and Margaret giggled.

Ademi didn't look amused. "You have a new boyfriend every week. I don't think that counts as news any longer."

With his head cocked, Enrique studied his manicured finger-nails. "I can't help how irresistible I am."

Ademi's expression grew sterner. "It doesn't count as irresistible if you manipulate their emotions."

The pout that scrunched Enrique's face made him look even hotter somehow. I wasn't sure it was solely his empathic ability that kept the men focused on Enrique. He said in his own defense, "I can't always help it. If I'm attracted to a man, my emotions kind of latch on to them as well."

Finally breathing normally after his dash from the parking lot, Rodney shook his head in disapproval. "You know that's an excuse. We've all been working on how to control what we can do so we don't hurt anyone else or remove their free will."

Ademi added, "Or hurt ourselves."

Now *that* I could relate to. I had a much better grip on my emotional empathy, but very little on my healing ability.

"So what do you expect me to do?" complained Enrique. Though my itchy scalp told me how irritated he was, I didn't need the extra help since his feelings were clear with his tightly crossed arms and bouncing foot. So I closed off my empathy just a bit by thickening the walls around my mental barrier. I'd gotten so good at constructing the thing every morning, that I barely remembered it was there, and yet it still worked.

Ironic that I learned the technique from this group and Enrique still refused to use it. "Have you been practicing your mental barrier?"

He dropped his head behind his chair and let his arms fall to the side. "It's so boring. How empty and gray everything feels when that barrier's up."

He wasn't wrong but missed the whole point. "Sure. It's a bit quieter in my brain but it's a lot easier to get work done without spiraling into someone else's bad day."

Rodney brought home the point. "What happened when that poodle owner had a temper tantrum?"

Reluctantly, Enrique met his gaze. "I lost it too and painted the dog pink."

Margaret covered her mouth. "You did not."

Ademi didn't let him stop there. "How did that work out for you?"

Belinda put a comforting hand on Enrique's shoulder. The young man dropped his attitude and rubbed his face with both hands. "Not well. The social media campaign wiped out 15 percent of my business. I probably would have lost all of it if that asshole hadn't been caught drugging his dogs to perform better at the show. His loss of reputation saved my business."

Proving why she was the right person to take over leadership of our group, Ademi knelt in front of Enrique and made him look her in the eye. "So you have to do something. If the mental barrier isn't working for you, then we need to try another technique."

There were other techniques? Maybe something would suppress the aggressive healing ability. Heidi could handle it just fine after all, but she didn't have emotional empathy to balance as well. "I could really use another technique too. I've been wholly unsuccessful with suppressing my healing ability. We can learn together, Enrique."

After brushing his cheek with the back of his hand, he

nodded. "All right, Ademi. What have you got in your bag of tricks?"

Chapter Four

Belinda and I stood on the sidelines of the miniature pitch while the six-year-olds on the team warmed up. The heat was sweltering, and it wasn't even noon. How did those little ones not collapse out there?

"Ever been to a wee soccer game before?" I asked Belinda.

Her face was flushed with heat as she shook her head no. Beyond the obvious discomfort from the temperature, Belinda exuded happiness. Belinda's joy while surrounded by so many strangers and children tickled my toes and fingers—something I homed in on to block the anxious anger from the overly committed dad next to us. She certainly seemed to enjoy crowds much more than I ever had.

On the pitch, my youngest nephew carefully aimed his foot at an unmoving ball, bit his lip, then kicked it without looking up. The ball flew past his partner, who watched it go by before realizing he should probably go get it. As much as I didn't want children, they did possess a certain amount of charm—or at least amusement value.

I leaned toward Sparrow. "You have a backup plan for his future scholarship, I hope."

Tori gave me a stern look as she waved Justin over to help

him with his shirt. I pictured her mothering him throughout college and into the pros. Yep. I could totally see it. Bless little Justin's heart, he was so short his light blue uniform shirt hung down to his knees. Justin was too busy holding up his shorts to worry about his shirt anyway. That boy was undoubtedly adorable, but I wasn't sure soccer was going to be his thing.

Sparrow shrugged, not reflecting the consternation emanating from his wife. "Whatever keeps them busy. And we're already saving for college. By the time they're ready, both boys can go wherever they want."

"Of course you are." I ruffled his hair. "It's a marvel you turned out so normal."

After Tori sent Justin back out to the field—with a corner of his shirt already escaping—she ran her fingers through Sparrow's hair to straighten it out from my disrespectful ruffling. "Hawke" —she emphasized his name as if I was just about to call him Sparrow out loud in front of their friends—"looks after his family. That's how he shows his love."

Offended for no good reason, my hackles rose. Belinda touched my elbow. Her amused look made me smile too. First, it was nice to be touched without absorbing someone's emotional state. Second, my brother getting praise didn't mean I was being dissed. *Calm down, Fauna. It's not all about you.*

"Dad! Mom! Uncle Bertram is here." Cooper ran up to his parents with Emblyn and Emmett right behind him, cheeks just as pink from their run. A few steps behind came Uncle Bertram in business casual attire, much too formal for the outdoor setting or the heat, with that newsboy cap solidly in place. Yet, he didn't look flustered at all. He squeezed the brim and tilted it at us like we were in some sort of period piece.

Cooper begged, "Can we go play?"

I interrupted Sparrow before he could finish. They couldn't run off before Belinda had a chance to tell me if the Ems were empaths or not. "How rude. Let me introduce my friend Belinda first. Belinda, these are the twins I was telling you about, Emblyn and Emmett."

Tuned in to Belinda's emotions on purpose so I could gage her assessment, my fingers tickled, but my gut tightened as well. Her face scrunched and head tilted, verifying the curiosity I was reading off of her. She couldn't tell, just like Forrest.

Belinda smiled at the children and reached out her hand to shake theirs one at a time. Surely after touching them, she'd have an answer for me.

Emblyn said in her sweet voice, "Nice to meet you, Belinda."

"Same," Emmett said when it was his turn to shake.

With my ability open and listening, a bit of fear emanated from Emblyn and Emmett who kept glancing at Bertram as if seeking approval.

Before I could follow that string, Sparrow sent the children off. "You three can go play as long as it's all right with Uncle Bertram."

Cooper jumped to see Bertram over the Ems, instead of simply leaning to the side. Oh, to have such energy. "Can we?"

Though Bertram wasn't close enough to read, his raised eyebrow told me he wanted to know if I'd found an answer. I shook my head. He laid a hand on each of his children's shoulders. "Maybe we should watch some of the game first. We are here to see Justin play after all."

Cooper collapsed to the grass. "But it's so boring. All they do is run back and forth."

As if to thwart Cooper's complaints, a soccer ball bounced right off his head and flew toward Belinda. She ducked and grabbed the Ems' hands as if to pull them down with her out of danger. The emotion Belinda felt changed to satisfaction. Before Cooper had time to complain, Belinda released Emblyn and Emmett's hands. She turned to me with a huge smile on her face.

"That's a yes," I said as much to confirm what I read from her as to inform Bertram that his suspicions were accurate.

Unaware of what was happening between us empaths, Tori

handed a juice box to each kid. "You don't have to watch the game. Stay hydrated and I'll expect you back here in an hour. Set your watch."

Sparrow helped Cooper set his. "With these flying soccer balls, it's probably safer in the woods. Go have fun and avoid the poison ivy, please."

"Leaves of three, leave it be." Cooper chanted as the three ten-year-olds ran down the path toward the manicured tree line.

"Cub Scouts?" Bertram asked.

Sparrow nodded. "He'll be in Boy Scouts soon. You should consider signing Emmett up."

Tori perked at the suggestion. "Yes, please. And we could get Emblyn in Girl Scouts. There's a troop at the school, and I've wanted to volunteer for a while. It would be nice to have some estrogen around here."

With her eyes focused on the fleeing little empaths, Belinda looked wistful. I whispered to her, "We'll talk to them later. Let them have fun for now. We have this riveting action to get back to anyway." One kid threw himself on the ground in a crying fit because a teammate had taken the ball from him. "Just like the pros."

Even Tori laughed at that one. My wit would win her over eventually.

⁂

WHEN THE GAME restarted after their cute little break of popsicles and water, I started to wish I had some cherry vodka for the juice box Tori had given me. The constant blocking of super-heated emotions, along with distancing myself from the gorgeous blonde who sneezed a lot, had worn me out.

Just as I gestured to Belinda for an escape, Cooper, Emblyn, and Emmett came screaming across the pitches, ignoring the shouts of parents and refs as the three interrupted games. Without hesitation, Sparrow took off to meet them while Tori rounded up Justin. Man, those parenting instincts were no joke. Uncle Bertram moved quicker than I'd ever seen him, but certainly not at an undignified run. Still, I had to jog to keep up with his long legs.

Upon closer inspection, only Cooper shouted. The Ems remained eerily quiet next to Cooper's reaction.

Sparrow held Cooper's shoulders looking him directly in the eye. "What happened? Are you okay?"

While his father inspected him for injury, Cooper's face practically steamed and was as bright red as the opposing teams' uniforms. My first instinct was to hand him the rest of my apple juice. When our hands touched, my gut clenched so painfully I dropped to my knees. Whatever Cooper had seen, it had terrified him.

Belinda helped me up, her eyes as wide as a spooked horse. A glance at the twins told me they didn't reflect the same terror.

Bertram nodded toward the tree line and simply said, "Show me."

"No, no, no." Cooper cried and folded himself into Sparrow like he had when he was a toddler.

Sparrow scooped him up. "Let's go see your mother."

After receiving a nod of agreement from Belinda, I said, "We'll go with them to see what happened."

We followed the twins beside my uncle under the trees. Why was Cooper so scared while the Ems showed no emotion at all? Had they done something to him? Belinda must have picked up my flash of anger aimed at Emblyn and Emmett. Her pinched lips and quick head shake admonished my accusation without me having to voice it.

The forest replaced the smell of sweaty children with the fresh scent of pine needles and something else I couldn't quite identify. "What is that?"

Bertram stopped so quickly in front of me I tripped, and he caught me before I dropped to the ground. When our skin touched, mine vibrated all over. How in the hell was Bertram feeling hopeful right now? He looked at Belinda. "The twins empathic abilities. Are you sure?"

What odd timing for the question?

At Belinda's nod, Bertram said, "You both should go. I'll take care of them."

This time fear pulsed from the Ems as they reached out and held each other's hands. I was missing something big, and there was no way Bertram was going to get me to leave before I figured it out.

"I'm not leaving until I find whatever scared Cooper so badly he couldn't even talk about it." I walked around Bertram and nodded to the twins. "We're away from everyone else. Tell me what happened."

Emblyn said, "It's better if we show you."

Emmett added, "It's this way."

Their actions felt cold, and I had no heartburn indicating guilt or tension in my throat indicating anxiety. What happened that left Cooper terrified, Bertram oddly hopeful, and the Ems turned off?

Right behind the Ems, Bertram and I breached the tree line to a paved path following a mostly dry creek. The sound of trickling water floated in the air.

With her brother right beside her, Emblyn dashed down the path about fifty yards to a fallen tree that made an impromptu bridge across the creek. "We crossed over here."

When we balanced across the natural bridge—Belinda on all fours like a raccoon—the unidentified smell intensified to the point that I knew exactly what it was. Bertram must have picked up on it too because we looked to our right at exactly the same moment. In the overgrown bushes that hid the view from the path on the other side was the mostly burnt body of a woman, melted upside down to the trunk of a cypress tree. Part of her dark hair had escaped the attack as had bits of green cloth that stuck out in odd angles.

Belinda took one look at what we'd already seen, and she scurried back to the other side of the creek.

While I fought my own nauseous stomach at the smell of charred human flesh, my body swelled with warmth from Bertram who called the twins to him before they got closer to the body. I didn't know what was going on, but I knew who I needed to call.

Luckily, he picked up right away, "Flores? I'm sorry for bothering you on a Saturday, but there's been a homicide."

Chapter Five

An active crime scene was becoming way too familiar. It wasn't exactly how I'd imagined my life. Flores conferred with his partner, Collins, who looked just as happy to see me as usual. Collins was convinced I was part of some sort of conspiracy, a la the *Blacklist*. As many times as I came across dead bodies, I really couldn't blame him. I'd gone my whole life without seeing a single one until a little over a year ago. Now I seemed to be surrounded by them.

A glance behind me showed the ones I loved dragged into this. Though technically Cooper and the twins had found the body, it still felt like it was my fault they were involved in this mess. The cops had found a purse with an ID for a Ginger Chan, but there was no way to visually confirm the identity based on what was left of her face.

Apparently finished with Collins, Flores came to me with his notes app on his phone open. "You know the drill."

"It's really sad I know the drill."

The stern cop facade Flores wore during these moments slipped just a bit, but it didn't stop him from doing his job. "Who found the body?"

If only I could lie and say it was me, but the Ems and Cooper waited for their turn to be interrogated. Best to just tell the truth. Plus, there was no way they were involved. It would just be a blip in their childhood. At least I hoped so. "Cooper, Emblyn, and Emmett came down here to play. I guess lots of kids come to throw rocks in the water while they're waiting for the games to finish. They crossed the creek on that fallen tree, and that's when they spotted her."

Through the trees on our side of the creek, Pradock and his forensic crew came through the underbrush with their equipment. Collins held up the police tape so they could get in.

"I know you don't want to do this part, but I have to question the children." Flores's matter of fact attitude helped keep me centered. "You don't have to come."

Not only did I have to come, but I wanted to ask the questions. "Of course I do." I was halfway to Cooper before Flores could say anything else.

The ten year old stared down the embankment, robotically tossing pebbles into the trickling water. I knew he did everything in his power to not look in the direction of the dead body, but I'd bet the image was seared into the young boy's mind. The Ems, on the other hand, fidgeted under Uncle Bertram's hovering form. They were more afraid now than when they had brought us to the victim. Yet, they didn't display any hesitation to stare at the body, which they did off and on every time I looked their way.

I didn't have time to sort through what any of it meant right now. It was time to do this horrible volunteer job I signed up for.

My throat choked up as I sat on the ground next to my nephew so I could look up at him. He'd lived the ideal family existence until now, and I had to be the one to shatter it. "Cooper, there are some horrible people in this world. And we have to do what we can to make the world better. Which means you tell Mr. Mateo what you saw, and then you can go home."

Sparrow stepped up, his strength and love smoothing out my

twisted insides with warmth. "Just tell him exactly what happened. You have nothing to fear."

Jaw set with determination, Cooper looked so much like his father. "I was looking for poison ivy to warn them what it looked like when Emblyn and Emmett ran off. I searched everywhere. I finally found them, but they didn't answer when I shouted their names. I perfectly balanced the log and then . . ." He pointed in the direction of the body but didn't look that way. "They just stared at it."

It was all too much, and I couldn't take it. I stood and took a step back, relinquishing the interrogation to Flores. I didn't want to do a reading on my nephew. It felt intrusive, especially when I knew in my heart the boy wouldn't lie about a thing. Instead I waved to Belinda on the opposite side of the embankment. She refused to come to the side with the murder victim. I didn't blame her. Though I did feel guilty that she was stuck here because I was her ride. I should have sent her home with Tori and Justin.

Belinda jumped as a man carrying a girl in a burgundy soccer uniform scooted around the trees and pushed his way through the gathered onlookers. "Ginger?" His frantic call demonstrated his panic, even though I couldn't sense anything from this far away.

Flores motioned for me to follow, as he balanced his way across the tree.

Up close, all I felt was worry from the man. The little girl showed no fear.

In full detective mode, Flores questioned the man with the kid. "What's your name, sir?"

He blinked like he'd never been asked that question before. He really was nervous. "Jason Chan. My wife's name is Ginger."

Flores asked, "What was your wife wearing?"

"A green tracksuit." His voice wavered like he was on the verge of crying, and he kept looking over Flores's shoulder to the other side of the creek like he sensed Flores held him back from seeing something. I'd never felt so grateful for Kudzu-covered underbrush. "She likes to come down here and get her steps in while Maddie plays. What happened down here?"

Too much to just be a coincidence. Between the ID and the missing wife with the same name and the green bits of fabric on the body, the victim had to be Ginger Chan.

I jumped when Belinda tugged at my elbow. Even the quick touch caused my shoulders to burn indicating her loathing. What in the heck was she hating right now? Oh please let it not be me. But she raised an eyebrow and shook her head in a quick back and forth movement. I swore that woman could read minds, not just emotions. She gestured toward a man I hadn't noticed before.

He bounced on his heels like he'd been out for a run, which his short shorts and sweat-absorbing T-shirt supported. But if Belinda found the man interesting, there had to be something more there.

As casually as I could, I nudged Flores and gestured to the suspicious man. Luckily, the jogger seemed distracted by the police presence on the other side of the creek and didn't pay any attention to what we were doing.

Flores pulled over a uniformed officer and had him get the contact details of the husband who paced in a tight circle rocking his daughter. Then we turned to the man who now leaned across a rotting tree trunk like he was stretching, but his neck strained to see what was happening on the other side of the creek. Something must have cued him to our approach because he quickly stiffened and stood up straight, staring right at us.

"Not today. It's too hot." Flores casually lifted his phone and took a picture of the suspicious man. "Don't run. I have your picture, and it won't take much to identify you with it."

The jogger's muscles were still tense, but he hadn't made a decision before we were close enough that Flores could have tackled him if he'd attempted to sprint off. "Can I see your ID please? We have to log everyone who was at the scene."

Sweat beads blossomed from his forehead as the man smiled nervously. "I left my wallet in the car. I'm just out for a jog and was curious. What happened?"

Belinda stomped her foot and crossed her arms. I couldn't help but smile at the thought of Belinda playing the bad cop. If she sensed something about this man, then I had to read him.

I stepped forward and offered him my hand, which he accepted. "I'm Fauna. don't worry about the detective here. He's just doing his job."

Most people simply shake back out of social training. It came in handy repeatedly when I needed a quick reading. As soon as we made contact, his nervousness tightened my throat until I almost couldn't breathe. This was one of my least favorite sensations, and it proved he was definitely hiding something. But it didn't mean he had any connection with the murder.

"I'm Richard." After Flores's eyebrow went up, Richard added, "Baptiste."

I released his hand and nodded to Flores. I didn't know if this man had committed the crime of murder, but he felt guilty about something. And I needed to step back and catch my breath before I vomited. At least this time, I was far enough from the crime scene to not soil it.

Flores asked Richard, "If you'll follow me please, I have a few questions." I'd seen Flores do this with suspects in interrogation rooms, confronting them with evidence to gage their reaction, but never at an actual crime scene.

Even though Richard looked like he'd rather do anything else, he quietly followed behind the detective. I gestured at Belinda, but she shook me off. So I followed the two men to get a clear reading. I wanted this murder solved and solved quickly, so my nephew and cousins could move forward with the healing part.

I had barely jumped over the last rugged root when Richard turned to the side and vomited directly into the creek below. Not only did that indicate innocence, it also set my stomach to queasy. It was much too hot for these smells to mingle in the air. I needed to sit down. A smooth boulder half in and half out of the mud—one good rain, and it would tumble into the creek below—would have to do as a resting spot for now.

As I got situated, trying to find a fresh breath of air, my hand brushed against the side of the stone where someone had left an impression. *Here I go again. Straight into the mind of a murderer.*

Chapter Six

My gut clenched as the anger of whomever left the impression took over my body. After all the practice with the Collective, I was much better at separating my experience from that of the memory leaver. But this anger was so intense that my everything tensed with it. I managed to push aside the physical discomfort in order to focus on what the person was doing.

The voice was young, maybe masculine, but it was hard to tell. He didn't look down at himself, so I had no idea what he looked like or what he wore. "Where are they?"

Straight ahead, a woman wearing a bright green tracksuit waved around a designer purse—just like the one the techs found the wallet in. So this was almost certainly connected to the crime. "I don't know who you're referring to. I'm looking for my daughter, Maddie."

That wasn't what the husband had said she was doing down here. Why the lie? Oddly, she had the top of the track suit unzipped and a very fancy lace bra peeked through. That's not what I would choose if I was going for a run.

The young, angry person kept talking. "You can't keep track

of your own child, yet you're responsible for the safety of others."

"I can't talk about a case with you or anyone." She crossed her arms. "Besides, I don't know what happened after the court date."

"And you got your money." His anger flared until my insides burned. "Well, if you refuse to help, I can't have you telling people I've been asking."

"What can you possibly do? You're not armed." Ginger scoffed.

"I'm always armed." He threw his hands up and waves of flames followed. I didn't see anything in his hands, but the anger was so fierce and the heat so piercing, it could have been anything. Well anything that could produce fire like a flame thrower.

Ginger flew through the air in a whirl and smashed into the tree upside down. Either the hit knocked her out or her death came too fast because she didn't scream, even as her track suit darkened to a deep brown and her skin bubbled. The fire faded as quickly as it had started, like it had used all its fuel in little more than a heartbeat.

Within the memory, a familiar voice called in a theater whisper, "Ginger? Are you over there? I've been looking forward to this all week."

The murderer on the stone tilted backward until he could see across the creek. It was Richard the not-jogger on the other side, which meant he definitely knew the victim. It also meant he might have seen the murderer.

I ripped my hand from the spot before the memory repeated. Watching a woman burn to death once in a lifetime was already too many times. I didn't want to experience it again. My body was engulfed in such a high level of internal heat that the scorching July air felt cool.

"Are you okay?" My body jerked as Bertram put a hand on my

shoulder. "Fauna, you're burning up. Stay here and I'll get you some water." His concern was endearing, but the confirmation that the heat I felt was real, not just a memory, frightened me. Nothing like that had happened before.

Before I could do more than offer a grateful nod, Flores was by my side. "What did you see?"

I would never take for granted this man who believed me without question. And there was no reason to hide anything from Bertram, who already knew what I could do—at least this part of it. "The man was asking about children. And Richard over there was meeting Ginger for something he was super excited about. He said he'd been waiting all week."

"Is he the guy?" Flores's skepticism hollowed my chest, but it was weak.

"Definitely not. But he might have seen the murderer."

Flores recognized that I was fine, and he released me and turned back to Richard. I was glad he didn't ask me how it happened, because I still couldn't figure that bit out.

Bertram handed me a cool bottle of water.

I drank deeply. The refreshing liquid didn't hiss when it touched my lips, which surprised me as much as anything else I'd witnessed today.

Bertram asked, "The victim's name was Ginger Chan?"

Not until I dropped the empty bottle from my lips did I notice that Bertram was nervous and the Ems hadn't taken their eyes off of him. Though I didn't trust everything I was feeling at the moment since the heat thing had me off balance, I swore they were afraid in a way I hadn't sensed from them when they showed us the dead body. What was going on here?

For a moment I wondered if that voice from the impression was Emmett's.

Where the hell was my mind going? There was no way a ten-year-old did what I just witnessed. The creepy image of both twins simply staring at the burn victim and Bertram believing they set the fireworks off at the BBQ added up to some frightening conclusions.

Before I could fall down another rabbit hole, Bertram offered me a ladder. "Why don't you come by the house this afternoon? I think we have a few things to talk about."

"More than a few."

Chapter Seven

For my first time at Bertram's house, I was a bit let down. I expected a huge mansion a la the Remington Estate. Instead, Bertram lived in an upper-middle-class neighborhood in a home that probably still cost twice as much as my modest townhouse but was certainly not a mansion. Bertram opened the door before I lifted my knuckle to knock. How did he know I was there? My mind searched for supernatural explanations instead of the camera over the door, which I immediately spotted.

My world went from me being the only empath to everyone must have some sort of ability. Surely I'd eventually find balance, right?

"Please, come in." Bertram opened his home like he would to a formal visitor, not his niece. "The twins are upstairs. I told them to rest after the ordeal they just went through."

The wrought iron–lined stairs curved up to a second-floor walkway open to the rest of the first floor. I couldn't hear anything from up there. Whatever Emblyn and Emmet were up to, they remained quiet about it. I wasn't ready to confront them, anyway. I had questions for their adoptive father first.

Bertram guided me to the formal dining room that was decorated more like a little sitting room. "Helga's preparing lunch. Are you hungry? I can have her make you a sandwich too."

"Helga?"

Bertram smiled like he was about to explain something very simple to a child. Was it normal to want to smack your uncle? "Helga takes care of us. She's here six days a week to clean and prep our meals."

Uncertain how to react to a servant, I didn't try that hard. "Sure. I'd love some lunch."

Not until Bertram mentioned food did my stomach assure me that it was empty. A crime scene had a way of taking away an appetite, but I was getting used to them and recovered much quicker than I used to—which made me a little sad.

"I'll go tell her. Have a seat and make yourself comfortable." He moved through a connecting door that had to lead to the kitchen.

The sudden emptiness left too much room for thoughts to swirl around in my head. Were the Ems involved in Ginger Chan's murder? Why were they afraid, and why was that fear always aimed at Bertram? Why was my uncle hopeful when he discovered the dead body? Bertram had recognized the victim's name. How were they connected?

The very scale of what I had to discover exhausted me. A fluffy, floral-printed chair called my name. It wasn't at all something I'd expected in the home of a bachelor, but he was now a father so maybe he tried to soften the place. Or maybe he hired an interior designer. The hung curtains and mis-matched furniture that somehow perfectly blended together as one statement of tranquility supported the latter. Disregarding the sticky sweat that had solidified when I entered the air conditioning, I fell into the fluffy chair.

A sharp pain stabbed into my hip as if the chair demanded I not put my dirty body within its confines. Tucked between the cushion and the side was a blue-painted wooden train with a happy face on it. I was pretty sure it was from that old kids show narrated by Ringo Starr. Were these toys still popular? As I reached for it, a vibration filled with fear and pain radiated to my fingertips.

I jumped up from the chair as fast as I could. My fingertips still tingled from the energy of the memory. How did I not feel that until I was right on top of it? My senses still went numb if I worked them a lot in one day, like an overworked muscle. My regular use had strengthened it, but everything had its limits.

With my head cocked, I stared at the train now partially sticking out of the cushion. The blue paint bubbled in places, and the back end was scorched. The train had been in a fire. That was one too many coincidences for me to ignore. So curiosity won over fear, and I pulled the train from the chair.

Immediately regretting my actions, I plunged into a smoky room lit only by licking flames. The woman whose memory I experienced ducked through a half-opened window to drop a toddler next to another one outside, both wore nothing but diapers and expressions of shock. They didn't cry; they didn't run. They just stood and stared. It reminded me so much of how the twins reacted to the sight of Ginger burned on the tree.

"Run!" screamed the woman. "I have to get . . ." A coughing fit ended her sentence. So I was in the memory of the toddlers' mother. The flames kicked up in intensity until she knew the back of her was blistered. "Go!"

The pain was so intense, I knew the woman wouldn't have been able to move at all if it wasn't for the adrenaline pumping through her system. When the toddlers clasped hands but didn't move, she bent forward to fall out the window herself. Before she got more than the hand that clutched the train toy through, the window flew open so hard it slammed into the frame and bounced back down, shattering. It was too much for the woman. With her wrist crushed in the fallen frame and her lungs filling with smoke, her panic became mine. Separating myself became more than I had the energy for; I couldn't breathe, and my chest ached while my skin hissed and peeled.

As flame engulfed her now-numb body much quicker than I thought possible, her last words escaped little more than a whimper. "I forgive you." She stared at the toddlers as she collapsed and released the train.

Back in Bertram's sitting room, I collapsed in front of the fluffy chair also having dropped the train. On the bottom in clear lettering was the name *Hayward*. Luckily, the heat quickly dissipated from my body, not like the one at the park where it lingered. Those toddlers had to be Emblyn and Emmett. I was in their house and no longer believed in coincidences.

When he saw me sprawled on the floor, Bertram set down the two plated sandwiches on the coffee table and rushed to my side. "Are you all right?" He helped me into the floral chair and picked up the discarded train. "This is the only item the twins had on them when I found them."

"It was tucked in the cushion." I wasn't in the mood to describe everything I saw, so instead I asked, "Did their mother die in a fire?"

Bertram handed me a glass of water that I practically gulped down while he spoke. "She did. And I think the twins started it."

They were just babies. How could anyone so small cause such damage? Yet, it was hard to deny what I'd just seen and their mother's last words: "I forgive you."

My skin was sensitive as if I suffered from a severe sunburn. The sensation was very different than what I experienced at the park where my insides burned. I was supposed to be proving that Emmett didn't commit murder. Instead, I find circumstantial evidence that this wasn't the first.

After handing me a plate, Bertram sat across from me in a straight-backed, striped chair. "Before you go too far in your conclusions, they were babies and had no idea what they were doing."

I stared at the plate for a second before setting it down. I'd lost my appetite again. "They're not babies now." My conclusions were heading exactly where he thought they were. "How often do they start fires?"

Belinda had confirmed the twins were empaths. There was no need to question Bertram's claim. She'd never been wrong, even when she tried to tell me Michelle, my brother Forrest's ex-assistant, was an empath and I didn't catch on. Yet fire starting sounded so sci-fi, it was hard to swallow. But reality had taken a turn a while back; why would it return to a sense of normalcy now?

Bertram nibbled on his sandwich. "That's the thing. They hadn't started any fires for years, not once. I began doubting whether they could do it at all until the fireworks went off the other day. I know Hawke thought it was his boy, but I believe it was the twins."

Even if the Ems had something to do with this, Bertram knew more than he was admitting. "When Flores said the name Ginger Chan, you reacted. How do you know her?"

A shake of his head later, Bertram answered, "Elizabeth—that's their mother—contacted me about her children. She believed there was something different about them and wanted my help."

Now that was a revelation. "How did she know to call you?"

"I was looking for you. So I'd put ads in cryptic magazines in search of gifted humans. The popularity of the internet made it much simpler, and I finally found some headway." He got up and went to the little bar on the wall bordering the kitchen. "It is, after all, how I found Hawke, but before that, it was how Emmett and Emblyn's mother contacted me."

The thought of him searching for us, but not until after Mom had passed, ate at me. "Mom was terrified of you."

"And I'll never know why. I have no idea what my brother told her. She was like you, you know. She could sense others' emotions."

Which also meant she could tell if someone was lying. So whatever my father told her had to have been the truth.

He raised a bottle of scotch with a question mark. It was mid-afternoon; I was dehydrated; I should have said no. All of this real talk required a bit of liquid numbing though. I held up two fingers horizontally, and he poured generous amounts into two crystal tumblers.

He stood next to my chair rather than sitting back down. "When I got to Elizabeth, it was too late, and she was gone. The house was burning, and the twins played on the sidewalk with that damaged train. I knew I couldn't leave them there. So I took them in."

The scotch made me bold. "That's all very heartwarming, but where does Ginger Chan come in?"

"Emblyn and Emmett lost their mother and father in that fire which left them without a representative. Ginger Chan is a child advocate, and she was assigned their case."

Well crap. So there was a connection. "Why would the twins want to kill her?"

Bertram shook his head, and I clearly picked up on his curiosity with my tingling fingers and tightened gut. He truly had no idea. While I had him close and was reading him this clearly, I asked, "Do you think the twins killed Ginger Chan?"

He simply said, "I don't know."

Yet, my chest opened and my body vibrated with positive energy which creeped me out more than anything else I'd learned that afternoon. Bertram was hopeful. He wanted it to be true. Why would he want his ten-year-old wards to be murderers?

Chapter Eight

This rollercoaster of a day wasn't over yet. At the bar of Guard and Grace, the manzana punch warmed my insides but did nothing to calm my nerves. The smart thing would've been to take a nap before my date with Tucker, and I tried. Between the murder scene this morning, the revelations at lunch time, and the shadow Michelle left behind in the corner of my bedroom, I wasn't able to get a wink of sleep. Michelle's stupid aura thing, a side effect of her invisibility gift, had proven impossible to remove. Out of desperation, I'd brought in a spiritualist who "cleansed" my home with burning sage and some chants. The aura hadn't budged.

As I waited for Tucker to arrive, I took in my swanky surroundings. We ate out on a regular basis, but rarely somewhere so posh. Grateful Tucker had warned me to wear something nice, at least I felt like I fit in, especially since I could wear high heels again. My toes would kill me by the end of the night, but my legs looked incredible. Even my velvet gloves—too warm for July—didn't look out of place wrapped around my fancy drink. Not part of my everyday attire anymore, I decided I needed the extra protection this evening. I had no idea what Tucker would've been exposed to at the hospital, and I didn't want to avoid touching him because I couldn't stop the healing ability.

Going for a deep reading of Tucker might not be such a bad option. There was no way Tucker had chosen this place on a whim. The clientele was dressed to the nines and sat on navy blue, high-backed stools at the bar. This caliber of an establishment served two kinds of people: people who were in the uber category of wealthy and people who were celebrating something.

Though the Wickman's might technically qualify as uber wealthy with their generations of lawyers, Tucker made his own way in the world as a rebel ER doc. My forehead beaded with sweat. So either he was going to break up with me or ask me to marry him. He'd said multiple times he couldn't live with this committed but not progressing relationship forever. Was that it? Did he think I'd take the news better over wagyu steak and truffle risotto? Or had he decided to take the plunge and go for it. I flexed my left hand covered in my protective wear. Would the ring go outside the glove or inside?

How could I possibly get married if I still couldn't function in the world without donning armor? Escape was my only option. I signaled for the check and downed the last of the cocktail. Before the glass hit the bar top, I felt Tucker behind me.

His almost constant lust toward me hummed in my sensitive areas. Though flattering—and returned in kind—I noticed the comforting warmth I'd grown addicted to, the one that meant he loved me, was weak. So he planned to break up with me. Normally, I'd be relieved when a relationship reached this point. But I'd never had one last as long or feel as natural as it had with Tucker, and I wasn't ready for it to end. Depression hit me strongly enough that I was able to use it to bulk up my barrier. Right now, my negative emotions helped me block any others. I'd take whatever help I could get.

"Done already? How long have you been waiting? I'll get the next one." Tucker put up two fingers to the bartender, who nodded and got right to mixing.

Had to love a straight man who enjoyed a good cocktail. I couldn't let him go. Where would I find another? Shit, how could I win here? I needed him in my life. Reflexively I squeezed his hand, needing to touch him.

Squeezing back, Tucker looked down at my gloved grip. "It's been one of those days, huh?"

"A bit of a germaphobe" was what I'd told him about my odd protective gear. It had worked for Gina and Amelia for years, why not my boyfriend?

One day when we'd split a bottle of wine, he'd said he'd never seen a case of a germaphobe that turned it off and on. That was probably the moment when I should have told him the truth, ripped off the Band-Aid when our relationship was still new. Instead, I'd distracted him by unzipping his pants. Now I was about to lose the only man I'd ever loved. And I could not deny that was exactly what I felt for this sexy, hardworking, kind, generous man.

"Excuse me, sir." The host in his black slacks, white shirt, and gray vest called to Tucker. "Your table is ready."

The dining room we walked through felt like it should be on the top floor, not the bottom. Its huge windows reflected the light of the long brass tubes that hung from the ceiling. I wondered if they were meant to keep the sound down. But how exactly would metal tubes work in that way? One way or another, whatever they'd done to the place certainly made it feel intimate even though almost every table was full. The host sat us at a navy-upholstered booth for two and placed solid backed menus in front of us.

"Your server will be right with you." Before he'd gotten more than a step away, someone came and filled up our water glasses.

Our server, Gary, came right after and told us the specials. If this level of service continued, Tucker wouldn't have time to discuss whatever it was he wanted to talk about. This could work for me. I should ask about everything on the menu in detail.

Tucker cleared his throat as soon as we were alone. "You're wearing heels. You must be feeling great."

With my barriers well packed with my current swath of emotions and no glowy sign of illness with Tucker, I took off my gloves to tuck my napkin in my lap. "It's really nice to have a foot that supports my weight reliably, even when I'm torturing them in these cute shoes."

Though I barred myself from reading Tucker, he wore everything he felt on his face anyway. My nephews would know he was nervous as he studied the menu, avoiding my gaze. "That's the most impressive physical therapy I've ever seen, considering the damage."

"Um," I started but didn't know where to go from there. I was healed because Heidi used her ability; it wasn't medical intervention at all. "It was a little more than that."

With his jaw tight, Tucker set down the menu. "I know. Because I've never seen a scar so quickly dissipated before. I don't know what doctors you're seeing, but I can't pretend I don't know you are seeking help somewhere. And I certainly can't pretend that I'm not hurt that you wouldn't ask for my recommendations or even confide in me what you were going through."

Holy shit, he thought I was cheating on him with another doctor. The relief at the revelation thrilled me so much that my barrier weakened as I released some of that concentration with a healthy laugh.

And Tucker's anger came through like a bulldozer and cramped my abdomen. "You think it's funny?"

"No, no, I don't." The pain in my stomach helped center me again. He might not be here to propose or break up with me, but he certainly had vital questions he needed answers to. But how could I tell him what I was and not chase him away? Maybe if I offered a bit of truth, I could placate him and salvage our relationship—at least for now. "I'm not seeing other doctors, Tucker."

"Then how?"

Time for me to clear my throat. "Well, it's kind of ridiculous, and I hope you'll give me the benefit of the doubt. You've seen the evidence with your own eyes." I pulled back the neck of my blouse to display the smooth skin where my shoulder scar had been.

He leaned forward, his big eyes open and almost watering. "Tell me."

Moment of truth. Maybe if he could handle this bit, he could take it all in. "Heidi is empathic, like supernaturally. She can heal people if she touches them and concentrates on their illness." I waited a moment as Tucker took in what I was saying. "She healed my scar tissue."

He hadn't moved but his brow wrinkled in deep thought. "She healed me from the Wasting Sickness, didn't she? I swear I felt something *different* when she touched me in the hallway."

That was a good sign. He worked through his own experiences to make sense of what I was telling him. I would expect nothing less from this genius of a man. Time for a little more, though maybe not the part about me making him sick to begin with. "She did. She also helped the rest of the ill with her abilities."

Tucker sat back and crossed his arms. "I knew it couldn't be psychosomatic." Something else seemed to click into place as he tilted his head at me. "If she can heal people, why did it take so long with the patients here as well as the ones in the other cities? Could I take her through the hospital and have her heal everyone? I mean, this could change everything."

For a moment, I couldn't tell if he was mocking me. With a little effort, I reached across the table to touch his hand, which he offered as soon as he realized I'd reached for it. My body swam with sensation all over, but my chest felt hollow. That made sense. Tucker struggled with hope and doubt.

So I told him more. "When Heidi heals, it weakens her. It takes her time to recover, days usually. Unless she saps the strength from another, which is where the Wasting Sickness originated." His frown made me continue faster. "But that was Forrest's doing. Heidi didn't know he was offering her human batteries so she could keep healing." I squeezed Tucker's hand as I felt his anger rise. Last thing I needed was for him to hate my brother. "And Forrest thought the victims would recover. He had no idea they would stay weak, because Heidi recovers on her own, just over time."

Tucker squeezed my hand. "So you're not seeing other doctors?"

His lightened mood made my whole body float. "Why do I feel like you'd be less hurt if I was sleeping with another man?"

He kissed my hand, and my nipples swelled in anticipation. "Oh, don't be so sure of that."

All tension left my body as I realized, somehow, he believed me. Should I just confess everything or stay satisfied with this much connection? Confessing that someone else had super-powers was quite different from knowing the woman you had a relationship with had superpowers. When Tucker ordered a bottle of wine and some appetizers, I decided to enjoy the evening and leave the rest of the details for later.

"So," I began with the cinnamon from the manzana punch still warm in my mouth, "after we've indulged in these delicacies, should we head to your place or mine?"

"Mine," he said without hesitation. "But you're staying the night."

My first instinct was to balk at his demand. Yet, he believed me. Maybe there was a future here, something I'd never dreamt of before. Unsure of the strength of my words, I simply nodded in agreement.

Chapter Nine

When the title song from *Hamilton* woke me up with a start, it took a moment to orient myself. I was on a couch, but it wasn't mine. The lack of a coffee table and the mounted TV that was three times the size of my living room wall refreshed my memory. I was at Tucker's condo. The sun streamed through the blinds of the east facing windows.

Holy shit. I really had stayed the whole night. This was a scenario I didn't know how to handle. Leslie Odom Jr's voice ended, and Tucker's husky, sleepy voice took over. Before I had decided if I should join him in bed or sneak out, his head popped around the bedroom door, eyebrows close together. Completely raw having not done any preparation, his fear, mixed with a touch of anger, drifted directly to my gut where my stomach dropped then cramped.

"I'm still here." I stood up from the couch and let the throw I bought him for Christmas tumble off. Naked while the sun rose was not a thing I usually experienced. If I was going to be raw, I might as well get something rewarding out of the experience.

As I'd hoped, his mood took a quick turn into lust. When our moods matched, there was no better high in the world.

Tucker practically sprinted to my side and dived into my embrace. Even though we'd satiated our lust last night, we pawed each other like we'd been apart for weeks. Just as his finger found the right spot and we turned to tumble to the couch, he dropped his phone from his other hand.

"Shit," he said, annoyance lacing his lust, though he still gently tweaked my left nipple so I was not so bothered. "My sister asked me to pick up her kids. Dave's out of town, and she's already in the office."

Okay, well that was killing it. "On a Sunday?"

Tucker kissed me, but his excitement had already waned as responsibility took over. "She's got a big case with a parent accused of killing their kid's psychiatrist."

I wasn't done with him yet. I'd spent the night, the whole night. I deserved a reward. "Well, we have to shower, don't we?"

His excitement flared back in full force, and he lifted me. I wrapped my legs around his waist. "Indeed we do."

THE WICKMAN LAW office occupied four whole floors of one of the swankier skyscrapers downtown. Tucker had promised to drop me off after he grabbed his nieces and nephew. He led me through the less than grand backdoor entrance with the keycard Reese had given him for emergencies. For a moment, I almost told him I'd wait for him at the diner across the street, but I'd always been curious about the life he'd left behind to become an overworked, underpaid ER doctor.

Maybe it was the long hours she had to work. "Why is your sister here on a Sunday?"

Tucker shrugged. "When she has a client she's sure is innocent, she doesn't take much time away from the case. This one is some father accused of killing his children's psychiatrist because of a negative recommendation for custody."

If only I'd told him about my ability, I could offer to do a reading. I'd know for sure whether the client was innocent. Maybe he wasn't and Reese could spend more time with her kids.

When the elevator doors opened, a large desk with an even larger security guard behind it dominated a luxurious waiting room. The leather-bound chairs with beaded backs and wide arms bordered an Oriental rug that probably cost more than all of my furniture combined. A full-service coffee stand that looked like it was usually manned by a real-life barista was sadly closed. A full-sized wine fridge stood just on the other side, and it didn't look locked. It was too early for even me to grab a drink, though.

I couldn't imagine what Reese's hourly rate was if this was what her clients expected when they came in for meetings. If it weren't Sunday, I felt certain I would be severely underdressed in leggings, Tucker's Astros T-shirt, and the heels from last night. If this new part of our relationship was going to be a habit, I'd better plant some clothes at his place. I grabbed a pack of gum from the coffee stand to cover up my breath. I'd need a tooth-brush too.

"Good morning, Mr. Wickman," the guard said.

"Good morning, Harry," replied Tucker. "I'm here to pick up the angels so my sister can continue to work herself to death."

"'Angels' is not what Mrs. Wickman calls them." Security Guard Harry laughed with genuine joy. Everyone liked Tucker; they couldn't help themselves. "And your guest?"

"This is Fauna Young, my girlfriend."

Oh shit. I was about to meet Tucker's sister. This was a bad plan. I only put a Band-Aid on our problems. What if I liked her? It would hurt even more when we broke up. "It's nice to meet you, Harry," I managed to say with only a little shake in my voice.

After checking my ID, he pulled out a clipboard. "I'll just need you to sign in."

As I tried to spell my name correctly with my mind spinning

over everything that was happening too fast for me, Tucker asked Security Guard Harry to buzz his sister.

Before I could put together a game plan, Reese came around the corner and down a short hallway. "Thank you, Tucker. I need to cross reference the fire marshal's report before our interview tomorrow." Then she spotted me and one eyebrow—blonde and fluffy like her brother's—rose about an inch.

Tucker waved me over. "I suppose it's about time for you two to meet, considering I only met Fauna because Reese lost her computer."

"I didn't lose it. It was stolen from my car at a tee-ball game." Reese stood straighter and held her hand out for a shake. "It's nice to finally meet you in person, Fauna. Tucker talks about you all the time."

While Tucker blushed, I felt emboldened by the revelation. "Does he now?" As suspected, all I got from her was tension in my throat and an annoyingly itchy eye from whatever stress she held at the moment.

Before it got too awkward, three elementary-aged children flew out from down the hallway and tackled Tucker. "Uncle Tuck!" They yelled in unison.

A boy about Cooper's age and two younger girls, who I would have taken for twins if I didn't know better, jumped up and down next to Tucker.

He introduced them. "This is Charlie and sweet Kylar and the little one here is Judy."

The person who herded the kids out of the offices called to Reese. "Ms. Wickman, we got the burn report back from the expert. There are definite inconsistencies."

A fire marshal? Another burn victim? I was much too tired to contemplate what the odds were.

"I'm coming, Grayson," Reese called back. "Well, I need to get to work. It was very nice meeting you, Fauna Young." She turned to her brother and walked away at the same time. "Please don't give them any candy. They've been out of day care for a week and return tomorrow. They're hyped up enough as it is, and I need them to sleep tonight."

"Yes, ma'am." Tucker saluted as he walked the crestfallen children out with me sluggishly following.

Security Guard Harry beat us to the elevator to press the button. "You should stop by more often, Dr. Wickman. Mrs. Wickman is always more relaxed after she sees you."

Tucker's face turned mischievous. "Are you sure it's not because I'm usually here to pick up her demon children?"

"Hey!" Little Judy protested.

Her older sister, Kylar, patted her head. "Don't worry. Uncle Tuck's kidding."

As soon as we got downstairs, Tucker twisted a make-believe mustache and said, "Who wants ice cream?"

"Me!" the children screamed at once.

After meeting Reese for two seconds, I was sure disobeying her orders wouldn't end well for anyone. "Didn't mom just say no sweets?"

Charlie rebutted, "She said no *candy*."

Kylar crossed her arms and looked remarkably like her mother. "Ice cream is not candy."

Little Judy took my hand. "Plus, we won't tell her. Right, Uncle Tuck?"

"Right," he said lifting her up and directing us to the little diner across the street. "You don't mind a little detour, do you?"

My entire body ached with exhaustion, but I wouldn't miss this moment for the world. "I love ice cream."

Chapter Ten

The diner could have been featured on Triple D. It had bright red, vinyl-upholstered booths and slightly faded black-and-white linoleum tiles. The walls held memorabilia from all kinds of iconic Houston events: Houston Livestock Show and Rodeo, Astros at Minute Maid, Zoo Lights at the Houston Zoo, the Johnson Space Center, the Hobby Center. Yet, this diner was nowhere near a tourist center, not that Houston had a distinct tourist-friendly area. Maybe they were just proud of the city.

Inside, the hostess—Felicia per her name tag—chomped on gum as she counted out laminated menus, paper menus, and crayons without even asking us how many. "Follow me."

With a 24-hour diner that had opened in the '70s according to the sign, I couldn't guarantee it would be clean of impressions. And I didn't wish to be assaulted by someone's memory when all I wanted was to hang with the kids and Uncle Tuck. People tended to keep their feelings in check when they could be spotted by others. "Could we please have a booth by the big window?"

The hostess blinked at the mostly empty restaurant that didn't have the post-church crowd yet. "You can sit wherever you like, honey." With a wave of her hand, the hostess opened the floor to us.

Tucker pushed the kids forward. "Well, go on then. Choose one."

To my utter amusement, Charlie jumped in one booth while Kylar chose another. "Angels, huh?" I laughed.

While her older siblings argued, Little Judy pulled on Tucker's pants. "We should sit at that one. It's so big." She pointed to a round booth that wasn't by the window but it did have a clear view to the street out front. *Sure, let's sit at the big one where people like to conspire close together in all the mob movies. That sounds like a great plan.* It was time to put my barriers to good use.

Tucker gave me a side eye, and I nodded my approval. Who was I to argue with a five-year-old? Her uncle clapped his hands. "Brilliant as always, Judy. All right, you guys, to the round booth. Last one there pays for the ice cream."

I'd never seen little bodies move so quickly. All three were seated with their legs swinging before I scooted into a spot on the end. Once I detected no impressions, I relaxed.

Tucker collapsed on the opposite end of the semi-circle, so the kids were sandwiched in between us like they were ours. What a thought.

Felicia laid the plastic menus in front of us. "What can I get y'all to drink?"

Judy chimed up first. "Ice cream."

Kylar shook her head. "That's not a drink. She'll take a water, and so will I."

Charlie ordered his own. "I want a chocolate milkshake."

"Me too!" shouted Judy.

Kylar's face paled, as if she regretted her choice, but she wasn't about to change it.

"Make that three chocolate milkshakes." He winked at his niece, and she smiled with relief that tickled my toes. "And I'll have a coffee."

How was he so effortlessly good with the children? I could

barely give my nephews hugs without feeling awkward about it. If I was going to get through to the Ems, I'd need to get better at this.

When Felicia turned to me, I ordered a cup of coffee. "With a scoop of vanilla ice cream in it."

An amused smile lifted Felicia's lips. "That actually sounds quite refreshing. I might have one myself."

When she looked at Tucker to see if he wanted to change his order, he waved a hand no. "You will all be punished if I consume ice cream right now."

Charlie made a farting noise, and the girls giggled.

Once everyone had sipped their milkshakes and ordered food, Judy pushed a red crayon toward me. "Do you want to color?"

"I would love to." How could I say no to such a sweet request?

As I filled in a clown's nose, I felt Tucker's hand cover my free one. His warmth quickly dissipated any chill I got from the ice cream–laced coffee. It wasn't just body heat either. His love filled me from my toes to the top of my head. And this deep feeling wasn't just for me. He felt the same for his nephew and nieces. The children's emotions jumped everywhere, as they seemed to always do at that age—probably why I had such a hard time being around children. But every time they looked at their Uncle Tuck, that same warmth emanated from them. It was the most intoxicating thing I'd ever felt.

While analyzing my personal feelings, I realized Tucker looked at me and the children in such a way that made me sure he wanted some of his own. Oh shit, forget my big secret. This could be the deal breaker. I couldn't pass this empathy on. I might be learning to live with it, might even do some good with it. But none of that made up for the decades of pain and isolation I'd experienced. How could I do that to an innocent child?

Before my mind spiraled to a panic attack and I moved to the bar, a server saved me with our food.

Judy stared at her homestyle potatoes with a wistful look on her face.

I asked her. "What's wrong?"

"There's no cantsoop." And she said it exactly like that. It was adorable.

At one of the empty booths by the window, there was a full bottle sitting on the table. This was a problem I could solve. "I got you, girl."

After cramming a fry in my mouth and scooting out of the vinyl seat, I made my way to the ketchup. My wrist brushed the windowsill as I grabbed the glass bottle and the room plunged into darkness as I fell into an impression.

Dammit. I let my guard down and now I had to brace myself for whatever this person felt so strongly that they weren't embarrassed to do it in front of a window.

Whoever's memory I experienced, they stared out the window at the door of the law office. It was dark so I couldn't see much through the window except the light over the door across the street and the occasional headlights of a car driving by. Though not certain, I believed the memory was a man's—the way he sat with his legs spread and his elbow rested against the windowsill. His anxiety was as high as any I'd ever felt. For not the first time, I wished I could read minds instead of only sense feelings. Though the fact that my gut wasn't cramping showed how well my barriers worked. It was odd having the sensation of the memory without the full-on physical assault, but I could get used to it.

Now curious, I stayed where I was instead of pulling back to Tucker and the kids. A jingle from behind the man told me the diner door had opened. My gut tightened slightly as his anxiety spiked, and a man sat down in front of him.

"He's good to go," said the dark-haired man, who had a wicked scar on his left cheek. Because the owner of the experience I shared was not an empath, I had no idea what the newcomer felt.

"He better be, Willis. There's no room for failure. I cannot be connected to this thing." The anxious man's stern voice sounded familiar, but I couldn't identify it. I'd had this problem before. When I hear myself recorded, my voice sounds wholly different than what I hear when I'm speaking. I've found, it's the same for everyone. Hence, through the man's memory, the voice was slightly distorted. Besides, what were the odds that I'd find an impression left by someone I knew at some random diner downtown?

A hunched over man in all black opened the back door to the law office, casting a shadow that made the window opaque for a moment. In the reflection, the man whose memory I experienced put a cell phone to his ear and said, "Yes, 911. I just heard gun shots at the law office of Wickman and Wickman . . ."

Nothing else he'd said registered as my skin prickled and my blood pumped cold. I could make out part of the side of his face in the reflection of the mirror. But it couldn't be. It—it looked like my father.

Chapter Eleven

After a long afternoon nap and a grocery store run, I was ready for dinner with the girls. I'd been so busy this week, I hadn't cooked once. So maybe I went a little overboard. I needed something to get my mind off that impression, the one with my father. Because it couldn't have been my father. Plus, I had much more pressing matters to get to, like roasting these peppers.

The caramel, pudding-like flan was already in the fridge solidifying. The pop of the skin on the poblano peppers as I roasted them over the open flame used to be satisfying. After what I saw yesterday, it kind of turned my stomach. Enough so that I turned off the stove and tossed the peppers in the microwave with some water to steam instead.

After what Bertram told me about Emblyn and Emmett's parents and what I saw on that impression from the toy train, their behavior made much more sense. Yet if they could set things on fire at whim, why had they stopped for years and started back up? Was the move to Houston traumatic for them? And why would they target the child advocate who placed them in Bertram's home? They certainly seemed afraid of him. Was that enough? They were so little when Bertram took them in, would they even recognize the child advocate?

So many questions and zero answers.

As I assembled the empanadas, the monotony of the repetition calmed my mind. A knock on the door happened at the same time as the door pushed open.

Gina's southern accent made everything she said sound almost like she sang it. "Heya, girlfriend. It smells amazing in here." Especially since she started dating Daryl.

Amelia closed the door behind them with her foot since her hands were occupied with a pitcher of margaritas. She set it down on the island and plopped down on a stool next to Gina. "It does smell good in here."

Swallowing my sadness did not hide the eye twitching from my girlfriends' anxiousness. Usually Amelia would have crowded into the modest kitchen with me and grabbed glasses. Gina would have pulled plates down and set the table. After I'd accidentally drained a bit of Amelia's energy when she busted into my bathroom to save me from Michelle, things hadn't quite been the same between us. Of course, Gina had been informed of the whole incident, and she was also more cautious than normal around me. Everything had been pretty normal during the barbecue at Sparrow's house, so I'd hoped Amelia had gotten over her fear. Come to think of it, she did hang with Tori more than normal and ran off with Heidi as soon as she joined us. Maybe I only wished our relationship was back to normal.

While I pulled down glasses, Amelia asked Gina about her vacation. "How are your parents doing?"

Gina smiled, and her anxiety lessened. If we all had parents as loving as Gina's, the world would be a much better place. "They're doing great. The bull's probably in his last year so they're having a hard time figuring out what to do with him. Dad wants to keep him as a pet, but Mom won't hear of it."

I held up my glass in salute. "Here's to your dad winning one!"

We clinked glasses like old times, and it felt good. Gina said, "I hope so. Old Blue has done good by the ranch, but I don't see that they have room to house two bulls. It might be kinder to put him down instead of allowing some young stud to break through all the fences to take him down."

"Speaking of a young stud . . ." Amelia took a long sip of her drink and gestured for Gina to fill in the rest.

Gina decided to deflect. "Yea, speaking of a young stud, how's Tucker doing, Fauna?"

She was too much tonight. Daryl really must be good for her. "I met his sister today."

Amelia almost spit out her margarita. "You did what now? Are you finally getting serious?"

Nice try, best friend of mine. "Maybe I am."

While Amelia wiped her mouth, Gina stood and began setting the table. I resisted a tear as maybe just maybe they were coming around. They did, after all, accept that I was an empath almost too easily. I shouldn't be shocked that there would be a bit of pushback. Would the same thing happen with Tucker after he had time to sit on my confession about Heidi?

Feeling insecure, I shared another fear. "Though he looked so good with his nieces and nephew. So natural. I can't give him that."

Gina baulked at my self-doubt. "Why not? I know you and Amelia made that pact, but you're great with your nephews. I bet you'd be a great mother."

"I can't have kids. There's no way I'd risk passing on this burden."

"There's definitely a downside." Avoiding eye contact with me, Amelia refilled our glasses. "But then again, I wouldn't have my nice shiny promotion without that gift of yours."

I waved off her compliment, mainly because I couldn't internalize her reprimand. "You earned that."

"I did." She clinked glasses again. "But I wouldn't have gotten it if I didn't have something to blackmail Bob with. That was all you."

Gina cut a piece of empanada. "Don't you think you're the perfect person to raise a child with empathy? You know exactly what was so difficult for you. You'd know exactly what your child was going through."

She had a point. It was why Bertram said he adopted the Ems. "I suppose. Are you seriously eating that empanada with a knife and a fork?"

"What?" Gina unabashedly put a forkful into her mouth. "I can't help it if my parents raised me with manners."

"Ha!" Amelia laughed. "Says the girl talking while chewing." She took a dramatic bite with her fingers then used the rest of the meat pie as a pointer. "You know, Fauna, your children might not even be empaths. Sparrow doesn't have it, does he?"

I hadn't thought of that. "That's true. I guess I'd always felt like it was inevitable."

"First, it's Hawke. Ya'll need to quit being mean to him." Gina's face straightened out, and I knew she was about to use her teacher voice. "With my students, sometimes they're like clones of their parents and sometimes they are so different, even their biological parents wonder where they came from. You'll have no idea until those little buggers start to show personality."

I almost giggled. We were getting back to normal. "So quit worrying about stuff that hasn't happened yet. Got it."

Amelia clinked glasses with Gina and said, "Well, that was almost too easy."

Gina smiled. "Looks like we're the con artists now."

Too happy to take offense at any reference to my past, I nevertheless changed the subject. "Is everything set for our hardware run tomorrow?"

One of the corporate gigs I'd secured to keep Chipped in the black was at Amelia's company, Stratagem. I could do the job and save them money, but I knew that contract was signed because Amelia put her name on the dotted line. I hoped that wasn't a ding on my already shaky karma since I'd helped her get that promotion and then benefited from it. It wasn't why I did it, so hopefully the universe would give me a break. Heaven knew I needed one.

Ignorant to my inner turmoil, Amelia simply nodded as she chewed another bite of empanada.

"Excellent." Unwilling to let Gina slip the hook completely, I turned to her. "Now, about that new beau of yours."

Amelia joined in on my focused attention. "Yea, about that new beau. Do you want Fauna to do a reading?"

"No!" Gina protested a little too quickly, I thought. She stumbled through her next sentence. "He's thoughtful and smart and my dad loved him. I want him to stay perfect for as long as possible. I don't need to know all his dirty little secrets. I have some of my own after all."

Again, she looked away from me. I wasn't sure I'd get used to that. Time to pretend not to be offended. "Well, I'd still like to meet him. I promise I'll shake his hand with my gloves on if that makes you feel more comfortable."

Always the most protective out of the three of us, Amelia's expression turned skeptical. She'd probably feel better if I did a reading. "Look, Gina. If you don't want to know anything more than you already do, then we respect that."

Gina's shoulders fell and she looked as vulnerable as her young students. "Maybe if we get more serious, I'll take you up on it."

That counted as a win in my book. "Who's ready for dessert?"

Chapter Twelve

S tratagem was a study in contrasts compared to the Wickman law offices. Whereas the practice held multiple floors in a high rise in the middle of downtown, this modest business occupied the space of a retail store in a strip mall. As Amelia showed me around, I noticed all of their desks were a bit worse for wear and the chairs were in varying states of needing to be replaced. There were no carved wooden antiques or fine leather couches. This was a workplace not a show piece. I felt much more at home.

Amelia's company created and implemented software for nonprofits across the country. Nonprofits required quite different services from corporate America. And their budgets tended to be smaller. So Amelia had to do more with less on a regular basis. That was probably why she was the problem solver out of our group of friends. She was just so damn good at it.

Even though the place could use an upgrade, it was clean, except for an odd burning smell. "Is something burning?"

Amelia waved at the less than cutting edge computer systems on each workplace. "I don't smell anything, but I probably stopped noticing years ago. You're our hardware guy now; pretty sure it's your job to ferret out any odd smells."

Bantering with Amelia made me feel at home. "I'll add it to the bill."

"I would expect no less." Amelia continued the tour as if I hadn't interrupted. "And this is where our esteemed head programmer, Matthew Udelhoven, makes the magic happen."

She motioned to a side room with no window and a low ceiling. Four monitors were set up on the deep desk that looked to be a higher quality than the others I'd passed. My guess was the cheaper furniture couldn't handle the weight. This guy definitely embraced the genius programmer stereotype down to the pile of soda cans and candy wrappers. A young man I assumed was not Matthew, tossed the mess into a trash bag.

Amelia's face scrunched. My abilities were back to full strength this morning after their overuse on Sunday. So I took extra time to make sure I did all my prep work properly before leaving the house. Still, I opened the barrier a bit because everything felt hollow if I couldn't feel anything. Because of that, my fingers tingled and my gut cramped just slightly. Nothing was painful when I controlled it like this, it was more like the memory of the sensations that I interpreted immediately into the feelings they represented.

In this case, Amelia was curious. "Um, Arnold, where's Matthew?"

In a button-up that looked like a hand-me-down and a pair of Dockers two inches too long, Arnold continued to drop cans into the bag with a consistent clink. "He never showed up for work."

"We need him today. We're on deadline." Distracted, Amelia nevertheless maintained her business demeanor. "Fauna Young, this is Arnold Shortman, our star intern. He can show you the server room and the minor amount of equipment we have in the storeroom."

I held my bravely ungloved hand out to Arnold. "Nice to meet you, Arnold."

He loosely gripped my hand. "And you, Fauna."

The back of my neck burned, and I quickly released his hand. He felt a deep loathing. I didn't think it was aimed at me. We'd just met, and that kind of hatred took time to develop. Either he felt that way about Amelia or the world in general. Then Arnold dropped the almost full bag into the garbage can by the door. "I'll finish his mess later."

Ah, he must resent Matthew, like, fiercely. I wondered what the programmer had done to the intern. That was when I noticed the blinking monitor. "Um, Amelia, it looks like Matthew left his computer unlocked."

The hair on my arm prickled with Amelia's surprise as she joined me. "That's impossible. He added so much security after we hired him, it took half the staff over a month before they remembered all the steps to log in to their own desktops."

"It was like that when I got here." Arnold added a bit too quickly for my liking.

Amelia didn't seem to share my unease, but she also hadn't felt the loathing I had. "Fauna, give me a minute. I'm gonna ask our office manager to get ahold of Matthew and see what's up."

Suspicious, I looked at the desk Arnold had been clearing off. I didn't see anything of note, until my foot slipped slightly. On the carpet by the desk was a Post-it scribbled with letters and numbers that spelled *HotCh3353!!!*. The numbers and capital letters and punctuation reminded me of a password. Though if Matthew was so security conscience, I'd have thought he would have used something random instead of a recognizable word at all. And he certainly wouldn't have written it on a Post-it note next to his desk.

As I bent down to pick up the yellow slip of paper, Arnold rushed to my side and grabbed it. "Sorry. I wasn't done cleaning yet. Shall we go to the server room?"

Suddenly not wanting to be alone with the creepy intern, I struggled for an excuse to be anywhere else. "I need to figure out what Matthew was doing. Maybe he VPNed in from another location. Though it shouldn't have unlocked his computer—"

"Okay, look." Arnold's face fell, making him look too young to have an internship for college credit. And my breath caught in my throat from his panic. He reminded me so much of Emmett wrapped in that fear. "Matthew programmed some software for the foster care agency that handled my case when I was a kid. He refused to look something up for me, no matter how much I begged or how many favors I did for him. As I cleaned his office like I do every morning, I saw the Post-it with his password written on it. When he didn't show up, I logged in and tried to get into the agency's system."

He started to cry, and I couldn't help but feel sorry for him. It seemed I was surrounded by foster kids lately, between my cousins, my new employee, and now Arnold here. It was a miracle or a curse that my brothers and I somehow avoided the system growing up. We were, after all, prime candidates. Maybe it was because Mom made sure we were always enrolled in school and we always had food, if nothing else. And we weren't abused, just poor.

One way or another, I wasn't sure if I believed him. His emotions had jumped so much since I'd walked in the room, they almost felt forced instead of genuine. At the very least, Arnold wasn't in control of them. It had to be torture to not know where you came from. "It's all right. Maybe I can help. Show me what you found."

Arnold blinked for a minute as if trying to decide if he should do it or run. "Okay."

He leaned over me, and I felt his relief. But that loathing still clung to him. "It's the For Anna Agency."

A search turned up a file for an organization under that name. "It looks like Matthew had worked on the employee/volunteer onboarding and training process. He didn't have access to their client files. Have you tried contacting the agency and asking them for the information?"

As I scrolled the list of employees, Arnold had his phone out, and I swore he took a picture. He flushed; the intensity of anger matched that deep-down hatred he carried. That creepiness I'd initially felt about Arnold came back. There was something familiar about it. "Have we met before?"

Before he answered, Amelia returned and held onto the door jamb, as if it was the only thing keeping her upright. She exuded a sense of anguish that locked my jaw. Arnold squeezed out into the main office without Amelia giving him a second glance.

Before I knew what to say, I was up and helping her into the office chair. "What happened?"

"Matthew's dead. His house caught on fire, and he didn't make it out."

Her words lined up in sentence form, but I had trouble digesting them. Another death and another fire? How many times could this possibly happen a year? Were they all connected? It made me think of the death Reese's client was accused of and the child advocate at the soccer game. And the death of the Ems' mother. At least, they couldn't be attached to some programmer on the other side of town.

Short on words, I simply said, "I'm sorry, Amelia. That's horrible."

She blinked at me, not quite crying, but not totally okay either. Her grief burned the back of my eyes. "Can you ask Flores to look into it? Matthew didn't smoke, and he certainly didn't cook. It couldn't have been an accident. But why would anyone want to hurt him. True, he was a bit of an asshole, but in an overconfidence kind of way, not in a make everyone else around you miserable kind of way."

There were too many coincidences, and I couldn't reconcile them. It was time to talk it out with an expert.

"I'll call him now." We'd planned to meet today anyway.

Chapter Thirteen

The smoldering remains of a modest, one-story home brought back the feeling of burning flesh from the impression on the train toy. A shiver ran along my skin that had nothing to do with the cooler air from the fire hose spray. The water would evaporate quicker than the remembered pain—and that smell. Before my mind wandered to what Matthew Udelhoven must have experienced, I focused on the men at work on the scene.

While the muscular firemen wrapped up their equipment, I found it disturbing that I didn't feel a touch of attraction. What was happening to me? Normally, Amelia and I would be back and forth about the hot firemen. Something had changed inside me, something I wasn't ready to face. I needed a drink. From the deep sadness that rolled off Amelia, she also could use an alcoholic aid or two.

Flores came over with his phone out, full of notes I was certain. He reminded me of Columbo with his head bent over his pad. Well, if Columbo had been fit, Latino, and gay. The part he shared was his keen observation skills and his caring attitude. I'd spent more time with cops than I'd ever pictured in the past, and Flores's qualities set him above most—most human beings, not just policemen. I was so glad he was the one called to Albert Johnson's murder. I couldn't imagine where my life would be otherwise. I swiped a tear from the corner of my eye. I was heading straight from here to a bar. It had been decided.

Amelia took a step forward to meet Flores. "Is he really in there? Is it Matthew?"

The flash of hope hurt. The look on Flores's face told us the truth before his words verified it. "We can't know for sure until the ME verifies identity, but the wallet on the body is definitely your programmer's."

"Fuck, fuck, fuck." Amelia collapsed to a crouch halfway between hiding and fleeing.

When I reached out a hand to comfort her, she flinched. Okay, so we weren't there yet. "Amelia, I'm so sorry." For much more than the loss of her friend. Turning to Flores, I asked, "Is there any connection?"

He shook his head and shrugged his shoulders, his touch of frustration closing my throat metaphorically. "The fire chief says it looks like there was only one source for the start of the fire and it was directly where the body was found. And no accelerant has been detected on a quick inspection. He'll need to get back lab results to know for sure."

Amelia popped back up. "So this was an accident? Some freak event?"

Of course, she didn't know what we did. It was funny I hadn't even considered it an accident. Would my mind always fall on foul play? I would not have described myself as innocent before, but I was definitely more cynical than I'd ever been—and that's saying something.

Flores kept his business face on. "Do you know anyone who would want to hurt him?"

Amelia scoffed. "I know plenty of people who would want to put laxatives in his Mountain Dew, but no one who would burn his house down."

Time to tell Flores about the connection I'd found. "He did

work on some software for a foster agency. So maybe the victim from the park—"

Amelia interrupted me. "Do you have something to do with this?"

Her accusation was a dagger to my heart. "No, I don't even know what's going on. But your intern said Matthew refused to show him some files."

My friend, at least I hoped she was still my friend, crossed her arm and stared at the ground. "Arnold had been a little off since he came to work for us. Matthew took to him right away, but something happened between the two and Matthew locked him out."

So maybe Arnold had been telling me the truth. "He told me Matthew refused to share some information about the For Anna Agency."

A spike of shock flowed over my scalp from Flores. Did he recognize the name? When I looked at him, he shook his head indicating now wasn't the time.

Amelia studied her shoes. "Is that what he said? Arnold had grown super nosy about the nonprofit client lists but only those involved in the care of children. Matthew thought he was a pedophile or something. He swore that kid had already downloaded some information on a child psychiatrist, but he couldn't prove it. He changed all of his passwords and reported the incident to me."

Flores asked, "Can you give me the intern's full name and contact information?"

"Of course, but the kid's harmless; I'm sure of it. He's just a little damaged from his childhood in foster care. I suppose I have a soft spot for people with tough childhoods." Amelia snuck a quick glance at me. "His name is Arnold Shortman. I'll get the office manager to text you his details."

"Thank you," Flores said with a squeeze of her elbow. "We'll find the truth. And if someone is responsible for what happened here, we'll make sure he faces justice."

Amelia patted his hand on her elbow, then reached in her pocket for her phone.

Flores put his away. "There's not much else I can do here until we get the report from the fire marshal and the ME. And we've got that meeting with Pedro."

A quick glimpse at my watch surprised me with the hour. "It's about that time, isn't it? Can I ride with you?"

"Of course." He nodded toward Amelia on her phone. "What about Amelia?"

"She drove me. And I think she'd like her distance anyway."

Flores sighed but didn't push any further.

As we made our way to the other side of the police line to his Ford Fusion, everything that happened swirled in my mind. Usually, my troubleshooting skills were used to fix a finicky computer. Who knew those same skills were handy for solving crimes? Because more facts started to fall into place and there was no way they were coincidences.

"Amelia said the intern had tracked down a child psychiatrist and that was why Matthew locked him out of the system."

Flores unlocked the doors while looking at me. "Is that important?"

Closing the door was like shutting an oven. Breathing was difficult until Flores rolled down the windows so the heat could escape. "I went with Tucker to pick up his nieces and nephew from his sister's law office. She was preparing a case for a client accused of murdering his children's psychiatrist and there was a fire involved. I know the chances of them being connected are ridiculous, but ridiculous is what's been connecting my life lately."

"Well, with as much trouble as we've been having with getting information from Wickman and Wickman for Pedro's case"—what did he just say?—"I'm not sure how much any lawyer is going to share with us about a crazy theory. Let's find the psychiatrist this intern tracked down first and go from there. Fauna, did you hear me?"

Oh, I heard him. "The lawyer Pedro's accused of shooting worked at Wickman and Wickman?"

"Yes," Flores pulled gently into traffic, but I knew his attention was focused on me. "What did that name trigger?"

"That's Tucker's family's firm. I was just there."

Flores added, "Plus, that For Anna Agency is the one that Ginger Chan consulted with more than any other."

Even the biggest skeptic had to see a connection now. What was going on?

Chapter Fourteen

This was our first meeting since Flores got his cousin transferred from Huntsville to the jail downtown. It was all under the guise of making sure the cancer didn't come back. Down here, Pedro Flores was much closer to the Med Center. Maybe now that Tucker knew about Heidi's real ability, he could finagle some paperwork to get Pedro to stay down here longer. That trip to Huntsville was a bear. Though Tucker had no idea that I was the one who actually did the healing in this case. I really needed to confess.

Wishing we'd had time to grab a drink first, I followed Flores into the interrogation room where Pedro already sat with his new lawyer, Heath Williams. The old, South African man looked tired. He'd fled his home country to escape the unfair court system only to end up in America where the system wasn't much better. For some reason, he decided to stay and try to make whatever difference he could. Which was why he'd agreed to take on Pedro's case, even though he had nothing much to go on besides our claims that he didn't do it.

For some reason, the legal system wouldn't take my assurance that Pedro was innocent into consideration. Flores had, though. After I healed Pedro of lung cancer, Pedro also was onboard with me being present. Pedro thought I was some sort of guardian angel, a manifestation of his abuela here to protect him in death as she couldn't in life.

Pedro's face lit up when his gaze landed on me. "I'm so glad to see you again. I'm feeling incredible. I don't ever remember feeling this good."

Sometimes, I did do good. even if it was a trick I'd only recently learned. He looked healthy, plump, with color in his cheeks. "I'm relieved. You weren't looking quite so robust last time I saw you."

Flores laughed. "I think you mean fat."

"Hey, cuz." Pedro lifted an eyebrow with amusement I wouldn't expect to see in someone facing a life sentence for a murder they didn't commit. When you go from terminal cancer to youthful health again, it must change your perspective. "I need to put on some meat to keep my energy high to fight my case."

Heath nodded at Pedro. "It's good to see you again. Before we get started, I want to verify that you've agreed to have Detective Mateo Flores and consultant Fauna Young in the room. Neither are covered under lawyer-client privilege."

Too nervous to not make a joke, I added, "It's okay. We're going to get married and then they can't make me testify, right, Pedro?"

"Any day, Fauna, any day." Pedro's mood tickled my fingertips. But again, more like a memory of tickling than an actual assault on my senses. I used my empathy to enhance my experience instead of taint it.

Since I was closer to Heath, his confusion overrode Pedro's joy. "If you are marrying, then you should do that before we talk about the case."

Flores leaned toward Heath conspiratorially. "Pretty sure they were just joking."

"Ah," Heath simply replied. Good thing we needed his legal advice, not his sense of humor. I decided I should probably straighten myself out before Heath kicked me from the interview.

"I'm sorry, Heath. I'll behave, I promise." Just one wink wouldn't hurt. When Pedro returned it with gusto and Flores's happiness made my skin feel light, I knew we'd be fine. Now if only I could gleam some sort of information from the interview to help Pedro get out.

Heath chose to ignore our winks and got down to business. "I've read the file, but I want to hear it from you. Tell me what happened that night, Pedro. From the beginning."

Pedro settled back and crossed his arms. His emotions faded to a dull hum, probably because he was concentrating on the events, not on how they made him feel. I had no need to touch him to make sure he told the truth. He had no motivation to lie when everyone in this room believed him innocent already.

"I heard about the job through Willis Ponces."

Willis? Where had I heard that name recently?

Flores added, "Willis was attending his sister's quinceañera at the time of death."

While shaking his head, Pedro exuded anxiety for the first time since he sat down. "But he was with me outside the building."

Heath took notes in the margins of something he had printed out. "If that's true, then you"—he gestured with his pencil at Flores—"need to find a way to break that alibi. Another suspect will help alleviate the guilt piled on my client. What happened next, Pedro?"

"Willis said it was a straight-forward robbery of a lawyer working late. The man had gotten the kids taken away from one of our friends, and he paid us to seek revenge."

Heath waved his mechanical pencil in Pedro's direction. "Based on Orem Cranston's record, if those kids were removed from that home, they were better off elsewhere. He specialized in keeping families together, not splitting them up."

Pedro held his hands up defensively. "Hey, if I've learned

anything while trapped in here, there's more than one reality. I'm just going to tell you mine."

Heath conceded, and I bit my lip, impressed with Pedro's self-awareness.

"Anyway, robbing a rich lawyer sounded like a good way to make some easy money. Willis said the lawyer'd be working late and to make sure to get him to open the safe. So he gave me the gun as persuasion." Pedro looked at his hands as if he could do the moment again and refuse the weapon. "I wasn't new to firearms. They were a necessity in my line of work. So I smelled the slightly burnt spoiled egg of freshly shot gunpowder. I asked him about it, and Jorge said he'd recently acquired the weapon and wanted to make sure it worked so he shot it into an old chair in the alley. Sure enough there was an old chair in the alley beside the building. We were friends. We'd worked together for years. I had no reason to suspect anything else."

With a deep sigh, he continued, "So I stuffed the gun into my pocket. Willis pointed at the back door to the building and said they made sure it was open. All I had to do was take the elevator to the fourteenth floor and turn right after the reception desk. He'd be the only one there.

"Just like he'd said, the back door was propped open with a small piece of wood shoved in the hole preventing the door from fully latching. The place was empty except for some people enjoying happy hour at the bar on the first floor. I took the elevator to where I'd been instructed. The first thing I noticed when the doors opened was how cold it was, like frigid. If they had so much money to waste on the air conditioning like this, any modicum of guilt I might have had about robbing the lawyer faded quickly."

He might have been innocent of the murder, but Pedro's soul wasn't clean of all sin. The bitterness of those around him having what he didn't still flowed with his words. But whatever he might have done back then, he'd paid for with his prison sentence, and

I knew he hadn't killed Orem. I was given a second chance after all the harm I did; it was time to pay that opportunity forward.

"But when I walked into the only office with a light on, an old man lay on the floor bleeding."

My hand found its way to my heart as it palpitated. The image of Albert sprawled on his kitchen tile, his own blood a bath underneath him, overwhelmed my vision. I knew exactly what it was like to come across a murder victim. At that moment, I felt even more kindred with Pedro's experience.

Pedro rubbed his hands through his full head of hair. "Something snapped and my anger went straight to pity. I dropped to my knees and turned him over. But it was too late. The old man's eyes had already glossed over. Now panicked, my only thought was escape. I didn't take a moment to grab anything, just sprinted for the door. When I got to the elevator bank, policemen with their guns already drawn poured out. I would have ran to the stairs anyway, but I had no idea where they were. Instead, I just fell to my knees with my hands behind my head and yelled, 'I didn't do it. He was like that when I got here.'"

He laughed, the kind of sound that held no glee in it. "I don't even know why I tried. But when I saw Mateo, I thought maybe he'd believe me. He knew I wasn't a murderer."

Flores stared at the floor under the table. "I wanted to, but the evidence—"

"Was all planted!" Pedro yelled, his sudden anger clenched in my gut, but my barriers held off all but a wisp of discomfort.

Flores mirrored his anger, making it harder to keep it all at bay. "What did you expect? The way you were leading your life, the escalation seemed inevitable."

A guard knocked on the door, but Flores waved him off and settled his voice. "I believe you now, and I'm sorry I didn't see it before. I'm here to make it right."

Pedro stared at the same spot under the table, breathing deeply. For that moment I could see the obvious family resemblance. It wasn't just a physical thing; it was also a shared family history, much like my brothers and I.

Heath stopped writing notes and focused on Flores. "Your belief in Pedro's innocence is admirable, but ultimately not useful. We need evidence to convince the judge that we warrant an appeal."

That sounded like something I could help with. "What do we need to do?"

"I'm not sure you can do anything to help the case. I'll review the details of the trial to see if Pedro had ineffective assistance of counsel. That's our best bet based on everything else I've seen and heard today." Heath cracked his neck, apparently thinking. "Though if we are granted a retrial, another suspect could be invaluable at swaying the jury."

Flores stood and shook hands with Heath. "Find the real killer. Got it."

When I grasped Heath's hand, a glow spot popped up on the lawyer's liver. Shit. Do I heal him? Do I ignore it? Does he even know?

Apparently, I'd frozen for too long because Flores gently used my shoulders to steer me toward the door. Heath blinked at me as he sat back down.

I might have my emotional empathy under control, but I had a long way to go with this healing ability.

As soon as we got to the street, Flores asked, "Are you all right? What happened in there?"

"It's this damn healing thing. I can see every imperfection in a person's body, and I don't know if I'm supposed to heal them or tell them to see their doctor or if it's nothing at all but a bad sandwich they ate." I leaned against the brick wall. "I don't know how Heidi does it."

Flores pulled his keys from his pocket. "Did you ask her?"

Why did he always make me feel like an idiot? "Well no."

His lifted eyebrows as he opened the door to his Ford Fusion said everything. "So that's the first order of business, after we go through the evidence box."

The reference to evidence made me consider the back door to the lawyer office; it was the same one Tucker and I used. And the same one that the could-be-my-father man watched with Willis. Shit. That was where I'd heard that name before. "Do you have a picture of that Willis guy?"

Flores nodded as he pulled onto Main. "It's in the evidence box."

If he was the same dude, what would I tell Flores? I mean, the truth, obviously. Why was I even hesitating? Old habits die hard, and I was still working on my trust issues. If it was my father from that vision at the diner and he was somehow involved in this case, then at least my distrust in people I should be able to rely on was well founded.

I was so distracted, I didn't notice that Flores drove away from 1200 Travis. "Um, is the evidence not in the room of cages?"

Flores answered with a simple, "Nope."

Chapter Fifteen

Time to put that trust to the test as we pulled into Flores's driveway. I'd been to his house a couple times since we became friendly but never without Austin here and never for business. It felt weird blending different aspects of my life together like this. Nevertheless, my life wasn't exactly straightforward. This was just one more complication.

I liked to keep a neat house, but mine felt like a primitive dwelling compared to Flores's. I supposed being married to an interior designer had its perks.

Flores cursed as he ran into a banquet table in the corner of the dining room. "Damn Austin, always bringing home new pieces and moving everything around."

Apparently there was also a downside to marrying an interior designer. I tried to hide my amusement as I helped Flores with the large cardboard box he carried. "Only one box?"

His mood drifted dark. "You'd be surprised how little it takes to convict a man of murder."

I placed my hand over his. "We'll get him out."

Flores exhaled and pulled the lid off. Right on top was a crinkled paper bag. He set it aside and pulled out a stack of pictures.

As he flipped through them, I asked, "Why is this evidence

at your house and not in the room of cages?" The evidence room had an actual name, but I liked my moniker better.

At least it made Flores hiccup laugh. "After a case is disposed, we don't keep the evidence anymore. Usually it gets sent up state to be destroyed, but I requested it. I could never let go of Abuela's warning, so I wanted to keep it close, just in case."

He dropped a picture of a young Hispanic man with a wicked scar across his left cheek on the table. "That's Willis."

I picked it up and blinked in disbelief. "Okay, this is weird even for me, but I saw this man in an impression at the diner across the street from Wickman and Wickman when I had ice cream with Tucker and his nieces and nephew. He was with another man." I couldn't quite spit out the words that the other man might have been my father. I mean, it probably wasn't anyway.

Flores laid out the pics on the table. "Is he here?"

Not knowing whether I wanted him to be there or not, I flipped through the pics shaking my head the whole time. "I don't see him." Did I feel relief or disappointment?

"We do have this. Maybe something on here will trigger your memory." He pulled out the object from the paper bag he'd set aside.

Just when I thought things couldn't get any weirder. "What in the heck is that? How long ago did this case occur?"

The VHS tape Flores held up felt like a relic from a bygone era. "You'd be surprised how many surveillance systems still haven't upgraded to digital."

"Do you have anything to play that on? I don't have anything to play DVDs on anymore, let alone VHS."

A twinkle lit up Flores's eye. "Follow me." He dropped the tape in the box and lifted the whole thing.

Careful to avoid the newly placed table this time, he led me outside to the detached, two-car garage. A nod indicated I should open the side door since his hands were full. Okay, so he had an old VHS player in his garage. Why did we need to take the evidence box with us?

Flores blocked the door before I bowled right through. "Before I let you into my man cave, you have to promise to keep it a secret. I don't let anyone in here, not even Austin. He has the rest of the house; this is my one sanctuary."

My fingers went up in the three-finger pledge. "I swear I will keep your secrets no matter how much porn you have hidden within these four walls."

He shook his head as he moved out of the way so I could open the door. "If only it were that predictable."

As the lights flipped on in the windowless building, I knew exactly why he swore me to secrecy. Parts of the man cave fit the stereotype: dim lighting, an old, scuffed up recliner, a huge flatscreen mounted to one wall, a wine fridge full of beer. But one wall threw the entire thing off balance. Flores had managed to amass the largest collection of old VHS tapes and DVDs from the '90s and early 2000s I'd ever seen. There were the original Disney covers on *Little Mermaid*, *Beauty and the Beast*, and *Aladdin* among so many others. An array of cult classics of the same era from *Edward Scissorhands* to *Clueless* to *Encino Man* to *Ever After* to *Cruel Intentions* had an entire shelf. Another had stacks of action movies including *Independence Day*, *Stargate*, *Twister*, and *Armageddon*.

Finally, I found my voice. "Wow! You know you can get all of these digitally, right?"

"Actually, you can't." Was that excitement I heard in his voice? The tickling of my toes and fingers backed up my interpretation. "Like *Dogma* here. You can't stream it anywhere. If I didn't have this old VHS, I'd be out of luck."

I mumbled to myself, "Legally maybe."

While Flores busied himself with the multiple remotes to get the security tape ready to view, I marveled at this side of the serious cop. "I see why you keep this place to yourself. Austin thinks he married a down-to-earth realist with no sense of humor. This would blow his mind and challenge his belief that he's the artistic one in the family."

Flores stopped with two remotes in his hand. "You dug in deep there. I just don't want him to make fun of me for liking old cartoons." The grainy video popped up on the screen. "Some days I just need to sit by myself and hum along to *The Lion King*."

"Now that I can understand." It felt wrong to sit in his armchair. But I needed somewhere to plant myself so I didn't pace. A stool next to a work bench was too clean to be used for anything that required power tools. I chose the stool and focused on the video.

Flores narrated what was happening on the screen. "It looks like I left it right when Pedro enters the building. We were lucky to get the footage at all because the camera usually faced the front door of the diner for security reasons. Unbeknownst to the owners, the camera had been shifted earlier that day to focus on the law office door."

Well, that was odd. "Did you ever find out who shifted it?"

Flores shook his head. "Nope. The diner owner first told us his video wouldn't help because it didn't face the direction we were asking about. Luckily, we asked to see it anyway and that's when we found out it had been moved. Here look."

He stopped the tape and rewound it a few minutes. When he hit play again, the lens faced the diner door which a waitress opened while putting on her jacket. She looked below the camera and nodded, then moved down the street pulling her keys from her purse. Then the camera moved in a couple jagged movements until it faced the law office back door across the street.

"Did you ask the waitress what she saw?"

A tingle behind my eye told me Flores was annoyed by my question. "Of course. All she remembered was a well-dressed businessman. All we could figure was someone wanted us to see Pedro go into the law office. Or someone didn't want us to see who went into the diner and it had nothing to do with the murder."

As the video continued, nothing happened of note for the next few minutes. "Where is the alley Pedro said he met Willis in?"

"Unfortunately, it's off to the right of where the camera is aimed. So we couldn't prove his alibi was made up." He rubbed his face with both hands. "I assumed Pedro was lying. He was so good at it when we ran together, so natural, I thought he was lying about this too."

With my hand on Flores's shoulder, his regret coughed up a bit of heartburn for me. "You can't blame yourself. You did your job and followed the evidence. And now you have me."

He squeezed my hand back, and I'd never welcomed a smile so happily in my life. We watched the tape and saw nothing else until the cops pulled up and blocked the back door. Since they didn't go in, I could only assume the arresting officers went in the front.

After the cops cleared the scene, the tape kept playing while I nodded at the evidence box. "What else is in there?"

"The gun." Flores pulled out a plastic bag containing a small caliber handgun of some sort. Though working with the police, I had not become any sort of gun expert, and I hoped to keep it that way.

With my hand against the plastic covering the bag, I didn't feel any telltale vibrations. "It's clean."

"Well damn." While Flores dropped the gun back into the box, the video shook, garnering my attention. The police had left the scene, and the camera was being repositioned back to the I entrance. A server well passed her prime held open the glass door and gave whoever repositioned it a thumbs up.

"Huh." Flores had also been distracted by the screen. "I don't think I've ever watched this far."

A light reflected off the glass, and I could almost make out who was repositioning the camera. "Can you pause it?"

Flores did and followed my focus. "Well, he's tall, whoever he is, but there's no way to know if he's involved in any way. He might just be a Good Samaritan helping out the server."

"He might be or . . ." The picture was grainy and it was only a partial reflection, but I was certain who it was this time. There was only one man who would remind me of my father who wore that ridiculous hat. "He's the one I saw talking to Willis inside the diner and calling 911 when Pedro entered."

Suddenly all business, Flores squinted at the reflection just as the man gripped the rim and lifted it slightly toward the server. "I'll take the tape in to be enhanced to see if we can get a better image."

Inside, I knew he didn't need to get anything enhanced. This whole time I'd been afraid the Ems were oddly connected to the strange murders, now it seemed Bertram was truly to blame.

Flores's phone rang, and I welcomed the pause to give me more time to spurt it all out. A lifetime of keeping secrets made it super difficult to spill them.

By Flores's tone, it was obvious he spoke to Collins. Just what I needed, extra complications. "I can be in . . . Oh." His face blanched and the hair rose on my arms at Flores's surprise, then his worry crawled along my scalp like an entire colony of ants. "I'll drop Fauna off and be right in. Yes, I have her here." He turned away from me, as if I couldn't hear him if he couldn't see me. "I'm well aware of how you feel, but she offers something I can't get anywhere else." He hung up with finality.

My arms squeezed my body in a hug, while I waited for Flores to spill the bad news. "So what happened?"

"Michelle escaped from custody on her way to court."

Chapter Sixteen

The shadow of Michelle in my bedroom felt menacing again. I'd spoken to both Forrest and Heidi, who assured me they were almost in Arkansas, far away from Michelle's grasp. I talked Forrest out of turning around to protect me. I couldn't see Michelle coming after me, not after what I did to her. Plus, Flores insisted on posting a uniformed officer outside my complex just in case she decided to show up and take another chance. The worst part was I knew how she escaped. She'd used her shadow ability. If I visited the area now, I was sure there'd be a relic of her left behind, just like the one in my bedroom.

My mind spun with possibilities. Everything else took energy. Surely, fading away did as well. Though I'd picked up on the healing ability that seemed to come naturally, I hadn't tried Michelle's disappearing act. There was something creepy about going invisible. All I could think of was teenage boys using the ability to spy on girls.

Before my thoughts spun into a deep black hole, I retrieved a too-cold bottle of Sauvignon Blanc from the fridge. One glass in, a knock interrupted my impending drunkenness. Fear engulfed me. Flores had a policeman outside, but they wouldn't see Michelle if she didn't want to be seen.

Thankfully, a man's voice called from the other side. "Fauna? Are you home? I heard about Michelle and think maybe you should come stay at my house."

I should feel safe with my uncle on the other side of the door worried about me. Instead, I felt off kilter. The reflection of Bertram's face in the diner window haunted me—as did the fact that I hadn't told Flores right away. Why would Bertram conspire with a felon to murder a lawyer? He solved his problems with money, didn't he? It must not have been him. There was more than one tall white guy who wore that hideous hat. Since he'd recently reentered my life, my mind just put his face in the reflection. Heck, I thought it was my dead father at first.

So I opened the door. "Hey, Uncle Bertram, Flores has an officer outside. I'm sure I'll be fine."

He walked in, and I couldn't help but feel tense as I waited for Michelle's shadow to sneak in at the same time. To my relief, there was no hint of her presence.

My relief was short lived as the delusion that the reflection might not have been Bertram faded. He gripped the rim of his newsboy cap and tilted it ever so slightly at me, just like he'd done to the server. It had been him. Before I could pummel him with questions, Bertram motioned to my bedroom. "Well, go pack some clothes. It's dinner time for Emblyn and Emmett, and I promised them Cousin Fauna would come by and join us."

My independent nature flared up. "I can take care of myself. I don't need protection." *Especially from an accomplice to murder*, I thought.

His smile was so disarming, like a kindly benefactor in an old black and white movie. Those were never quite what they seemed either. "I know you can, but you don't have to. That's why I'm here." His arms found my shoulders, and a sense of peace with a gentle worry behind it filled my soul.

I let out a deep sigh and acquiesced. The mention of the Ems made me realize who was really in danger here. I could take care of myself. How would the children?

"Okay. You win. But I'm cooking dinner."

"Deal." Bertram dropped his hands and pulled out his phone. "Tell me what you need and I'll have Helga pick it up."

Servants were such an odd concept. Considering how I grew up, it was surreal to have such a wealthy relative. Wealth or no, he had something going on, and I needed to find out what. And though he had something to do with the murder of a lawyer, he had never harmed me. The memory of my mom's fear of him ached at the back of my mind, but I hadn't been lying in my protest. I could take care of myself. A few nights at his house under the guise of protection from Michelle would give me the ideal opportunity to snoop around and uncover more evidence.

The distraction of the escape had given me the perfect excuse to not confess what I knew about the identity of the person of interest on the VHS tape. Now I had the opportunity to get more details and be able to present Flores with all the facts.

That was the plan, anyway.

Chapter Seventeen

A fter dinner at Bertram's, I gladly relegated the dishes to Helga, who seemed relieved that she hadn't had to cook dinner. Imagine never having to wash a dish again? That would be true luxury. A shake of my head reminded me this was a temporary gig. I needed to play detective, then return to my uneventful life. If there was a return.

In that vein, I'd made zero progress. I couldn't very well ask Bertram if he was a murderer with the kids present, and the Ems and I hadn't been alone for a second so I could ask them why they were so afraid. Out of desperation, I volunteered to get them ready for bed—even though I had no idea what kind of help ten-year-olds required. One way or another, it gave me an excuse to ask them the hard questions.

Bertram winked at me while I grabbed the hands of my cousins and headed up the stairs. He really did want me to talk to them, someone who understood what they were going through. How could I think this man who adopted two orphans with abilities in order to protect them could do anything so horrible as orchestrate a murder? Maybe he didn't know that was what happened.

Emblyn and Emmett exuded eagerness at having me there, at least as much enthusiasm as I'd ever seen them display before. It might have had more to do with the cookies I bribed them with, but I would take a win when I could get it. They had to open up to me. Without Bertram around, I hoped that would be something easier for them to do.

As we made it to the second floor and their adjoining rooms, I marveled at how untouched the spaces looked. The same designer who had a hand in the downstairs obviously decorated up here as well since they looked like they were pictures straight from an Abercrombie and Fitch catalog. Yet, I couldn't believe two ten-year-olds lived within. I'd seen my nephews' rooms plenty of times. They were just as immaculately put together, but there was always a sock sticking out from under the bed or candy wrappers hidden in a pillowcase or a full basket of dirty clothes. The Ems had been with Bertram for a few years. Shouldn't they be comfortable by now? I wondered what was holding them back.

Seemingly familiar with a nighttime routine, Emblyn set me down in a chair next to her side of the Jack and Jill bathroom while Emmett walked through the shared tub area to his sink. Images of the three Young siblings crammed into a tiny motel bathroom trying to brush our teeth over a sink too small to fit a cup under the faucet flashed through my mind. It was hard not to be bitter, even though my life was great now. These kids weren't born into this comfort, but they surely wouldn't remember anything other than this.

So why were they so afraid? The gripped stomach I'd felt all evening never loosened. They carried some sort of innate fear that seemed to intensify whenever Bertram addressed them.

Well, I had to start somewhere. "How do y'all like Houston?" Which was of course when I noticed my mistake. The Ems turned to me with toothbrushes in their mouths and blinked. "I'll let y'all finish, then we can talk."

Sitting still was not going to work for me. I got up to take a closer look at Emblyn's room. The bookshelf was full of picture books I was sure they were too old for. Either they were behind on reading, they didn't like to read, or they weren't consulted on what should be on their shelves. There was certainly nothing I'd call personal. While Emblyn and Emmett simultaneously closed their bathroom doors to change into pajamas, I took the opportunity to peruse Emmett's room. Nothing stood out unusual there either. It was as if the rooms were for display instead of living, breathing children. If these kids liked to start fires, there was no evidence of it in their personal spaces.

While I waited for them to change, unpacking my bag that Helga had left in the guest room seemed like the logical next step.

The room smelled of vanilla from the candle lit on the dresser. This room had one wall of floral wallpaper and hardwood floors with a handwoven rug under the queen-sized bed. Uncertain if I planned on putting my clothes in drawers or just using my suitcase as a hamper, I pulled open the top drawer of the solid wood dresser. It moved smoother than I would have expected for something so heavy. Through my barriers, something tickled my skin. There was an impression nearby.

Curiosity peaked, I pulled open the second drawer. It was empty. The third one at the bottom, however, was much heavier. Inside were adult horror books by Stephen King and Dean Koontz and Anne Rice, books I would consider for a much older crowd than ten-year-olds. Scattered among the disorganized collection were pieces of macabre, such as the skull of a small animal, a decaying log, and a half-burnt candle. The only bit that seemed to carry a memory was the same little wooden train with the burnt bits I'd sat on a few days ago, the one with the impression of the Ems' mom in the fire. Did Bertram bring it up here and stuff it in the guest room drawer? Why would he do that? He said he'd let the Ems keep it and hadn't been lying, I was sure of it. Plus, why would a grown man hide a secret stash in the bottom drawer of a guest bedroom.

My scalp itched and the pit of my stomach dropped. The Ems stood in the doorway and their anxiety practically rolled off of them in waves. It was the strongest emotion I'd sensed in them since we'd met and the first time I'd seen it directed at anyone besides Bertram. Not such a good way to start our conversation.

Of course. This was theirs. For some reason, they must not feel safe keeping anything in their room. I sat cross legged on the floor in front of the open drawer with my hands in my lap and looked at them with a tilt of my head. The non-threatening demeanor worked with frightened adults, why wouldn't it work with frightened children?

Emblyn blurted out, "Please don't tell Daddy Bertram."

Emmett pushed his sister into the room and closed the door. "We should have moved everything, but we didn't have time before you arrived, and Ms. Helga set up the room for you." His voice sounded angry, but his fear radiated from him like heat.

I had to ask. "What are you scared of?"

The Ems exchanged a look and locked their jaws. I had to get them to open up.

"You know, my dad died when I was very young, and my mom died when I was about your age now. I know what it's like to not have anyone to look out for you except each other. That's what me and my brothers did."

Emblyn seemed more comfortable than Emmett, and the words just poured out. "Daddy Bertram wants us to start fires. He's desperate for it to be true. He thought we killed that lady in the woods, and he was happy about it. But we can't."

Happy about it? Before I dived too deeply into what that meant, Emmett took over from his sister.

He sat next to me and pulled out the Stephen King *Firestarter* book. "We did research to try to figure out how it's done, but it's no good. We can't do it."

Emblyn sat on my other side. "We don't want to be sent away.

We want to make Daddy Bertram proud, but no matter what we've tried, we can't make a fire with our minds."

When Emmett reached forward to drop the book back in the drawer, I noticed a burn on his wrist. "How did you get that?"

Emblyn rolled a half-burnt candle along the bottom of the box, while Emmett explained. "We thought maybe if there was already a fire present, we could at least make it bigger. But all we managed was some unimpressive burns."

So they couldn't start fires. Still, Belinda sensed something in the twins. "You know, I can't start fires either, but I can do other things."

The Ems tilted their heads at the exact same angle, and I started to understand why so many horror movies used twins. Except I could feel their emotions, and my tingling fingers and slightly squeezing gut told me they were just curious, not psychotic. Which I must confess was a relief. Not only could they not start fires, but I didn't believe these children capable of malice of any sort. They were simply more contemplative and serious than the other children in my life. Trauma certainly changed my brothers and I, and we didn't see our parents consumed in flames.

Nevertheless, they had some sort of empathic ability. Belinda had confirmed as much. Maybe if they trusted me, they'd tell me what they *can* do.

"Can I see your wrist?" I asked Emmett, who didn't even hesitate to drop it in my open palm. Though I could see the charred skin with my eyes, the healing ability dove deeper. Highlighting in that weird glow, it seemed to prefer the deeper damage underneath. With a gentle push of the warmth within, my gift flowed from me and enveloped the damaged skin.

Emmett gasped but didn't pull away. Emblyn leaned over my lap to get a better look. "Does it hurt?" she asked her brother.

A smile brushed his lips, and I had to control the healing to stay on the burn as it wanted to climb up and fix the lip he apparently chewed on. "It tickles."

When the skin was fresh and pink again, Emmett manipulated his wrist in every direction, the joy uplifting my own mood at each twist.

To take full advantage of the points I hoped I'd just earned, I asked them what I'd been dying to know. "So if you two can't start fires, what can you do?"

The Ems smiled at me, then held hands. They both jerked their heads at the drawer, and it slammed shut. Unprepared for the sudden noise, I jumped to my feet. The train impression from their mother when the toddlers held hands and the window shot open came back in full force. They hadn't started the fire, but they had tried to get their mom out. Then who was their mother forgiving?

The warmth associated with pride that had radiated from the Ems morphed into severe heartburn when their heads dropped in guilt.

"Oh, no, no, no. Don't feel bad." I squatted down and put a hand on each of their shoulders. "You surprised me is all. That's pretty cool."

They dove into my arms, and I stumbled flat on my butt. Their relief didn't overshadow my true emotion. And I was so glad they weren't emotional empaths because I really was scared. What did this mean that these little ones could do something so unnatural? How many of these legendary abilities were out there? Where did they come from? And why had I never seen any of it beyond my own curse until recently?

Bertram's voice called from downstairs. "Are y'all all right up there?"

He knew more. He had to. "Yep. Just a little bonding before bedtime."

After an extra tight squeeze, I released the Ems. "All right, you two. We'll talk more later. For now, let's finish getting ready for bed."

They jumped up and sprinted for their rooms with the energy endemic of youth. I had to figure out what Bertram wanted with them. Something within blossomed in a way I hadn't felt before—protectiveness. Nothing would happen to those two, not if I had anything to say about it.

Chapter Eighteen

It felt so strange to stand in front of Chipped like everything was normal. Nothing was normal. Bertram was involved in a decade old murder. The Ems had abilities unlike any I'd seen. Tucker wanted a serious commitment. My head ached from the onslaught of problems in front of me. In only a few months, I'd gone from being pretty much alone to part of a community and a family I had to protect. How was I not to buckle under this pressure?

As my bare hand pushed open the door, I forced myself to take a deep breath. Things were changing, no doubt about it. But change wasn't always bad. Empathy was a blessing, not a curse, when I could go through life without wearing gloves and solving old cases with Flores. All I needed was a vacation to take it all in. Or just an earlier drinking time.

A quiet soul joined me on the sidewalk outside the store. Before she said a thing, I knew it was Maggie. "Good morning, Ms. Young."

With a push on the door, I motioned her in ahead of me. "Good morning, Maggie. And please call me Fauna. I may be your boss, but you're making me feel old."

She laughed as she typed in the alarm code. Her level of

comfort made me feel like I'd made the right choice in hiring her. "I'll try to remember to call my elders by the name they prefer, Fauna."

"Watch it, whipper snapper. A kindness offered is not grounds for insolence."

She raised an eyebrow at me as she flipped on the lights and turned the *closed* sign to *open*. "Yeah, that didn't make you sound old at all."

"Hey, watch it. Age and treachery will always win over youth and vigor."

She moved behind the register to activate the POS system. "Whatever you say, boss."

"Careful, you're starting to sound like Jeff." I handed her my bag to stow behind the counter. "Now would you be a dear?"

Maggie shook her head at me. "Of course. Anything to help age and treachery with my youthful vigor."

When I'd first hired her, she could barely look me in the eye. Now Maggie was comfortable enough to walk around me and turn off the alarm while keeping up with a gentle banter. Perhaps I could trust the store to her and truly take that vacation. The image of Tucker, shirtless, lounging on the beach taunted me for exactly three seconds before the door chimed.

Jeff and Linda entered with their infant daughter. Their joy was contagious, and I couldn't help but join in it. Maggie, on the other hand, seemed to close up. The peace I felt from her darkened and deepened as if she'd pulled herself out of the situation mentally.

When she spoke, that scared girl I hired was reflected in her voice. "Is it safe to bring such a young baby out in public?"

Unaffected by Maggie's inner conflict, Jeff's mood didn't change. "She just got her first set of shots. She's as safe as she's going to be."

Christine straightened her daughter's shirt when Jeff turned her around so she could look into the store. "Plus, she's our third, and it turns out they're not really that fragile."

Jeff held her toward me like the lion cub from *The Lion King.* "Fauna, meet Ashleine."

I had to resist the urge to bolt. None of my small group of friends had had children yet, and I truly didn't know what was expected of me. My nephews were born while Forrest and I still traveled from city to city. What if I dropped her?

Christine's gentle smile tried to comfort me, but it only made me feel like more of an outcast. "You won't drop her."

Was it that obvious? My head itched with anxiety. That was when I realized the down play in emotions I'd felt from Maggie was her nervousness around Ashleine. And I was reflecting the exact same experience back.

The look of disappointment from Jeff as I shook my head changed my mind. If I was to make a go at this becoming a better person nonsense, I needed to end this fear of children. I'd never help Emblyn and Emmett if I couldn't take the very basic steps toward caring.

My arms thrust out as if their eagerness to hold the warm bundle of joy was completely separate from my angst. Now that I could block all but the strongest emotions from taking over my own, I really had no legit reason not to relax and enjoy. Besides, I wasn't taking Ashleine home, just giving her cuddles.

Finally, I caved. "Come here, you precious thing."

Jeff tucked her into my arms. "She still needs a bit of support for her head, but not much. She's stronger and developing faster than her brothers did."

After he tucked Ashleine into my arms, he took a step back. Out of curiosity, I dropped my barriers to a minimum. What would an infant feel? My body vibrated with anticipation, then slight disappointment. Everything I got from Ashleine was, I don't know, primitive? Nothing hit home hard, yet nothing was completely empty either. It was like each of my muscles tickled or flexed and every nerve started to tighten, then stopped. So odd.

Then I really looked at her, and her whole body glowed. I

almost dropped her in surprise. She didn't pull energy from me, so she couldn't be ill. Right? And nothing shouted an alarm from any strong emotion. Maybe she didn't feel much emotionally right now because her body used all of its energy to grow. Certainly it would make all of this nonsense make sense if it was energy based. That's why my empathy stopped working when I'd used it too much or why Heidi couldn't continuously heal because it wore her out. Maybe that was what I saw with the little ones every time I hung out with children. It wasn't that they were all sick or anything like that; they were growing. Fascinating.

But Ashleine smelled like baby powder, and her soft skin brought me some sort of odd comfort. I rubbed her cheek with the tip of my finger. "You are quite the miracle, aren't you?" Thoughts of my mom invaded the experience. What had she felt when she held me?

When Christine leaned in to put back on a sock, Ashleine's subtle spattering of emotions focused on that warmth I got from Tucker when we were close—the same feeling I'd started to recognize in myself. Ashleine loved her mom. I thought that was the most complicated emotion of all. It was one of the reasons I avoided such relationships and why I didn't stay close with my family. Love was just too much. Maybe I was wrong about that. It turned out love was the most primitive and simplest of them all.

Christine backing up was about all the tiny human could take for one day. Her energy swirled in circles, almost making me dizzy, and she began to cry.

Jeff swooped in and hugged Ashleine close, leaving my arms more empty than they had been before I'd held her. "Okay, sweet girl. No bawling on the boss." He winked at me though his smile never faded. "Fauna's not so tight with kids, and Daddy needs this job."

Suddenly I didn't know what to do with my arms. What would a tiny Fauna/Tucker baby look like? Would she feel for me what Ashleine obviously feels for her mother? What the hell was I thinking about? I couldn't risk passing on this empathy. It didn't matter that I'd learned to cope better, I still wasn't okay, not near normal.

Now I knew what to do with my hands. "Thank you for bringing her by, you guys. She's precious beyond words. Now I need to get to vacuuming." A deep clean always did me good.

Christine held the door as Jeff carried their newest addition out. She looked back at me with a tilt to her head. "If you ever want to babysit, let me know."

It never stopped impressing me when non-empathic people could still recognize something inside another person. "I will."

Quickly moving to the back before I pulled out my calendar and set a date, I didn't realize Maggie had left the register until I found her in the break room pacing. A turn of my head confirmed there wasn't a duplicate still in the front. Before I could comment on how quietly she'd disappeared, Maggie's anxiety rippled through me, creating a phantom itch along my scalp.

"Are you okay?" I asked her, forgetting about my own anxious feelings.

Maggie halted mid turn as if she'd run into an invisible barrier. "Oh yeah, I'm fine. Just looking for the vacuum."

Rubbing one's upper arms compulsively was not a sign of fineness. "You mean that one?" I pointed to the vacuum two feet in front of her on the wall.

The poor girl's anxiety blossomed into full blown panic. "Yes, yes, I must have been distracted."

The playful bantering young woman had disappeared, replaced by a terrified little girl. I had no idea what had changed her mood so quickly. My brother had taught me skills to manipulate people's emotions based on my body language. Sometimes, those skills came in handy for good instead of evil. I sat down, leaned back in the chair, and crossed my legs to exude an element of calm for Maggie's sake.

"The floor is pretty clean." I left out the bit about coming back to grab the vacuum myself. Somehow the need to help Maggie overrode any nervousness sparked by an unpredictable baby. "Wanna talk about it?"

Slumped over the vacuum like a defeated warrior, Maggie rocked her whole body instead of simply nodding her head. Her body loosened up some as she sat across from me and laid her chin on her crossed hands on the table. "I don't know what's wrong."

At least she was trying. It was more than I did at her age. "Do you often have anxiety attacks like this?"

"Not anymore." Maggie stared in my direction, but it was like she looked through me, not at me. "It was something about seeing Jeff's wife with the baby. So loving, so there for her. I . . ."

She trailed off and didn't seem eager to continue. Maybe if I shared something, it would help. She hadn't had a background check done on me like I had on her. Time to even the deck. "My father died when I was young, and my mother wasn't exactly stable. My brothers and I had to make it on our own. Loving parents aren't given to everyone."

Maggie laughed with no humor, but she did finally meet my eyes with her gaze. "That's putting it mildly. I had no one, bounced around in foster care from one uncaring person to another. I was used as a paycheck or free labor, never treated as a daughter by anyone."

"But you made it out."

She sat up with her hands braced on the table. "I did. Thanks to Dr. Anderson. He was the only person who ever made me feel important. He listened when I talked and actually tried to make my life better. He was a child psychiatrist and had a room full of us he was trying to help." She brushed a tear from her eye, but I didn't sense sadness. Instead anger became prominent even though her voice remained steady, as if Maggie recited a boring story she had to memorize for an assignment.

I judged it best to let her talk in case something I said stopped her from continuing.

"Dr. Anderson asked us to call him Liam, but I just couldn't. He was more than four letters. At least to me he was, but I wasn't his only patient. That waiting room was a mess with one kid after another, fucked up in some way or another. Sometimes, I'd just escape out of . . ." Maggie froze, and I swore a bit of fear drifted through the anger. But it was hard to tell, it came in and out so fast.

Time for a little comfort. "That had to have been hard to finally have someone to care for you, but you had to share him."

She blinked at me, recovering from whatever had crossed her mind.

I prodded a little more. "Do you still see Dr. Anderson?"

That did it. "No one does. He's dead, burned to death in his office." Maggie practically shook with anger that vibrated so strongly, my face flushed. "One of the boys he tried to help, same age as me, set fires all over town. He even lit a box of tissues on fire one day in the waiting room. I'm sure he did it. I know he did it."

The world was full of injustice. And apparently coincidence. How many fire related deaths can one person be associated with? It couldn't be though, right? The world didn't work that way. The empath deaths weren't a coincidence. The Wasting Sickness among the homeless wasn't a coincidence. These fires had to be connected. Maybe this was the case that would put together the missing pieces. "I believe you. Can you tell me more about this kid? Maybe I can help?"

Maggie scrunched her nose and jerked her head back in doubt. It was the first time she truly looked like the young adult she was, with all the attitude that came with it. "How can *you* help?"

Ouch. The way she said "you" could have been classified as a weapon. *Calm your roll, Fauna. She really is just a kid and has no idea what you can do.* It wasn't like she critiqued my food or anything.

Now that would be unforgivable. "I've got a detective friend with HPD who could look into it."

She stood and pushed her chair in. "No reason. There's already someone's dad on trial. The cops did what they always do and found an easy person to lay the blame on then continued harassing people with speeding tickets."

"Someone's already on trial?"

"Yeah, rumor has it, he has some big-time law firm."

Something tugged at the back of my mind. "What did you say your doctor's name was again?"

"Dr. Liam Anderson."

I picked up my phone. Flores could find the name of the victim in Reese's case.

He answered on the first ring. "How did you know?"

I had no idea what he was talking about. "I'm just that good. Also, know what?"

Though I couldn't see his face, I knew the exact puzzled expression that came with the long pause. "There's been another fire death. This time at Wickman and Wickman."

Definitely not a coincidence. "I'll be right there."

Chapter Nineteen

When I got off of the elevator on the Wickman floor, the scene was quite different than it had been on Sunday. The peaceful professional space had turned into a crime scene. The smell of burned flesh and plastic permeated the entry along with anger, much like the tarot card reader from last year. Yet, nothing here was burnt. Whatever happened in the back-office area must have been huge.

Firefighters casually walked out of the back. At least the fire had to be under control since half their gear was unbuckled and their demeanor remained calm.

Oh god, what if the victim was Reese? As soon as Tucker found out I was involved in the investigation, would he ever look at me the same way? Those sweet babies would lose their mother just like the Ems had. My stomach churned, and I cursed at myself for not asking Flores immediately who the victim was.

I could probably scoot around the firefighters and see for myself. A few steps into the waiting room, one of the uniformed officers pointed to Flores who had his phone out taking notes. "Ms. Young, Detective Flores asked for you to wait here."

I nodded and recognized Security Guard Harry in one of the leather chairs with his head in his hands. If only I had super hearing or something, I could discern what they were talking about. Sweat stains blossomed under Harry's arms and on his chest, and beads dripped from his neck. That was quite a difference from the efficient man I'd met the other day. He held an ice pack against the back of his head. Whatever had happened had messed him up. I felt so helpless surrounded by so many damaged people. How did Flores deal with this case after case? I wasn't sure I was meant for this line of work.

Questioning whether I should have rushed down here, I leaned against the welcome desk. First lesson, I needed to be more careful what I touched when I came to these scenes because there was an impression embedded in the wood. Luckily, my barriers were under control, so I was able to read it without being possessed by it. Since I'd touched this desk a couple days ago and this impression wasn't here, I knew it had to be a fresh one. Maybe I didn't need supersonic hearing to find out what happened.

My mind became crystal clear and focused. It was nice to be inside a brain that wasn't frantic. At least it was until the intense focus morphed to anger verging on fury. Whoever's impression I was in stared at the security guard as if he could will the stubborn man to let him through.

From the corner of the vision, I could see a package held by two pale hands set on top of the welcome desk. "I have a delivery, and you can't stop me from dropping it off. My boss insists that it get delivered today."

The voice was familiar, as was the anger. This was for sure the person from the soccer field murder.

Security Guard Harry spoke. "I don't care who the package is from. You can't go to the offices without an appointment. We're not even open yet. Just leave it here and I'll make sure"—he leaned forward and read the name on the cardboard box—"Ms. Wickman gets it."

Oh crap, it was for Reese. I had to resist the urge to pull away and sprint to the back. No reason to start the impression again. Let's see it through first. If what I was smelling was any indication, it was too late to save her anyway. The least I could do for Tucker was find her killer. The reality didn't make my stomach hurt any less though, even as I fought the cramping of my gut from the impression leaver's anger.

The package handler said, "I will not take no for an answer, all right?"

His voice sounded casual, but his inner dialog spoke of intense fury. So much so that the air around him felt heated. It almost swirled against his skin like a warm breeze in July. The contrast against the freezing cold of the air-conditioned room sent goosebumps up my arms. Security Guard Harry must have felt it too because sweat blossomed under his arms and beaded on his forehead.

A tsunami of steaming air flowed around the delivery guy with such ferocity his hat flew off. His fingers gripped the package tighter as the wave hit the burly security guard and threw him against the wall as if he were no more than a doll. The loud smack made me wince, but the delivery guy didn't twitch at the violence. My breathing picked up its pace as Security Guard Harry slid to the floor, unconscious.

A head popped around the corner of the hallway leading to the back offices. I recognized him immediately as the man who had spoken to Reese about a report. "Is everything okay out here?"

The delivery guy's face cracked. Since I couldn't see him, I assumed the sensation meant he smiled, though I felt no friendliness from the guy—just that insurmountable fury. "Everything's great out here. I just have a package to deliver . . ."

The rest of whatever he said faded away as he moved his hands from the desk, still holding the package. Reality popped back into place, and I felt suddenly cold. And thirsty.

Flores raised an eyebrow at me, and I gave him an affirmative nod. We'd been doing this together for only a year, yet it felt so natural he'd already learned to pick up on my clues. I never would have been able to hide my abilities from him for as long as I had from my best friends. That same observation skill was also what made him a good detective.

"He called you, didn't he?" Collins, on the other hand, was seriously starting to piss me off.

I didn't have time for his anger toward me. Collins said he was trying to protect Flores, but he was just jealous that I figured things out he couldn't even fathom. Sometimes, people wait too long to retire. Collins should up his timeline. "Maybe he wanted a partner who could help him find the killer."

My voice wasn't loud enough to carry across the crowded waiting room, but Flores jumped to his feet anyway as Collins dropped his fists and his face flashed red. His anger felt pathetic compared to the fire starter.

Flores followed me through the hallway, pushing aside Collins's wordless objections as he passed his partner. "What did you see?"

"Some delivery guy threw the security guard against the wall then headed back to the offices." My blood practically boiled I was so angry that another fire took another victim and I was no closer to solving the problem. "This is getting fucking ridiculous. Don't they have cameras in this place."

"They all fritzed at the same time." When we reached the other side of the hallway, Flores grabbed me and pulled me into a niche between offices. "Are you okay?"

His worried look pissed me off. Why did everyone think I was a delicate flower who couldn't take care of myself? I was more than capable. Fury amped up my energy level as I prepared to . . .

Flores's concern overwhelmed the anger as if a tsunami of cold water drowned it. What had I been about to do? "I'm sorry." I offered, forcing contriteness I didn't quite feel into my words. "There's something about this place, something truly horrifying that's affecting me in a way I'm having trouble controlling."

To Flores's credit, he didn't run away screaming. He'd seen what I could do. But he did change his tactic. "Maybe you should go home. I'll let you know if we find anything."

With a bit more control as my blocks went up in a second layer echoing my mom's hymns into a cacophony to drown out the outside influence, I shook my head at Flores's suggestion. "No, I'll be fine. Just tell me the victim isn't Reese Wickman. She's Tucker's sister."

Flores's eyes softened as he reassured me. "The victim is a man, and he has no connection to the other fire-related crimes except maybe Ms. Wickman's current client."

As if summoned, Reese stormed down the hallway with a uniformed officer in tow. "This is my property, and I'm a lawyer. You cannot keep me from my files which happen to be located back here." She froze when she saw me. "Fauna?"

Chapter Twenty

The uniformed officer tried to do his job. "I'm sorry, but it's an active crime scene and—"

Flores relieved the poor man. "It's okay, Officer Thompson. I've got her."

Reese had pinned her focus on me and didn't waver. "What are you doing here?"

Even with my barriers up at full force, my chest felt hollow as it reflected Reese's doubt. Just what I needed. Tucker and I had started to get somewhere and now his sister would sow seeds of doubt in his already questioning mind. "Hey, Reese. Um, I'm sure Tucker told you how I consult with the police sometimes—"

"On cold cases." She crossed her arms and narrowed her eyes. "Though how a computer expert can help with this case baffles me. I saw no warrant to search any of our devices."

Collins unhelpfully stepped in. "Ms. Wickman, I presume. I'm Detective Collins, and I assure you, computer touching is not what Fauna does for us."

Somehow managing to suppress a groan, I tried to defend myself. "It's a bit more complicated than that." How awkward would it be if I confessed to Reese before Tucker. Maybe the work-around I'd attempted just wasn't enough. If I truly wanted things to progress with Tucker, it was time to dive in full force. After, of course, I dealt with the current situation.

Reese wasn't budging. "I'm sure it is. And I want this case solved immediately. But I can't let you into my systems without a warrant. And it better pinpoint exactly what you're allowed to have access to. Lawyer-client confidentiality applies to the digital age too."

All business, Flores said, "We're working on the warrants now. But anything you can help us with would be appreciated."

Collins asked, "Based on your case load, we know you represent a client who is being charged with murder in regards to the fire death of a psychiatrist."

I hoped they'd say the name of the psychiatrist out loud. It would tell me how far reaching this conspiracy really went, and the last thing I wanted to do right now was interrupt the interrogation.

Reese rolled her eyes in a way that somehow felt dignified. I wondered if she could show me how to do that. "Sure. It makes total sense to set fire to your lawyer's colleague to prove your innocence."

When Collins pulled off the doorframe to continue the argument, Flores gestured toward the opening. I took the hint and slipped inside. The completely drenched carpet from the fire repression system sucked on my shoes as took those initial steps. Unfortunately, their attempts had done nothing to stop the flames before they consumed the victim. I had to find something with my abilities, since any other evidence was likely washed away with the torrent.

Though I'd had a hint of it from the entrance and a preview with the woman stuck to the tree, the sweet and sour smell that hit me now made my stomach churn. The body laid half on the ornate desk and half on the floor like it was molded to the furniture. With my eyes closed, I took a deep breath in and out through my mouth. *I won't vomit. I won't vomit. I won't vomit.*

Officer Pradock praised an eyebrow at me. I waved him off.

He waved Flores closer. "This one is different than the park case. This victim was burned in sections, not in one big conflagration."

Curiosity settled my stomach. I wondered if the ease to which I stifled my nausea should frighten me more than it did. Something this horrific shouldn't become routine for anyone. For a moment, I understood Flores in a way I hadn't before. He had an underlying sadness about him, part of his overall aura. I had thought it stemmed from his past and his rocky relationship with his family, so similar to my own experiences. But maybe I'd been self-reflecting too heavily. Maybe it had more to do with what he was exposed to every day. He saw the very worst of humankind and yet he still wanted to raise children into this mess.

Something about that hope within such utter devastation made me want to make a better world for those kids. Even though I didn't really want to know, I asked, "What does that mean?"

Pradock didn't seem annoyed that I asked the question instead of Flores, who got down closer to observe what the crime scene expert referred to. "There's unharmed flesh below each knee and around each wrist. It's like he took a blow torch to each extremity that basically melted the man to the desk, then quick flashed the rest of him somehow."

Collins coughed, and I swore he swallowed deeply trying to keep his cool. "So the man was tortured before being killed. You only torture someone if you're looking for information."

Flores looked up with his head still aimed down in that way that made me know I was supported. I guess that meant I was on. Time for me to find an impression and maybe solve the whole thing. If the killer took his time with this victim, surely I'd get a good view of him. But the thought of diving into this man's pain, experiencing that kind of torment, scared the shit out of me.

After watching me waffle back and forth, Flores offered a way out. "You don't have to."

Oh yeah, he'd make an incredible father. Of course I had to. I knew the Ems couldn't be responsible now, but I still wasn't sure what Bertram's part in all of this was. Except he was at the house all night and saw Emblyn and Emmett off to school this morning. There was no way he was able to make it all the way downtown, murder someone, then get back in time for carline.

"I'll be fine." I reassured Flores and focused on the desk around the burnt flesh.

It looked familiar. Though the row upon row of file cabinets on the other side did not—unless you counted a show like *Warehouse 13*. That kind of organized and expansive storage would look right at home there. Didn't Wickman and Wickman believe in computer storage?

"I don't feel any impressions, but I swear I've seen this desk somewhere."

Flores nodded but didn't come any closer. "You would have seen it in crime scene photos. It's Orem Cranston's."

Oh shit. This was the desk of the lawyer Pedro was accused of murdering? The ghastly burned corpse half on and half off the desk made the deaths at least two for this piece of furniture.

Without looking up, I tried to comfort Flores like he always did me. "We're going to solve it you know."

"It's not just the desk. It's Orem's whole office. No one wanted to work in here after his death—superstition, I suppose. A superstition that proved accurate in this case." From the doorway, Reese held her hand over her nose and mouth but didn't flinch from the sight. I supposed she'd seen some pretty gruesome things in her day as well—in picture form anyway. "You know, Grayson wasn't perfect, but he didn't deserve this."

It hurt to think about, but with all of my experience with energies, why couldn't a room be cursed?

"So the perp walked in, bulled past the security guard, broke the cameras, and murdered Mr. Michaels." Flores remained focused and brought me back to the case at hand. "Yet, he didn't come across his intended target and nothing else is damaged."

Collins no longer bothered to stop Reese, who moved past the desk to the files behind it. "Intended target?"

Flores answered her honestly, "He came with a package for Reese Wickman."

"You mean this one?" She bent down and picked up a soggy box next to an open drawer with paper and manila folders strewn on the floor. "I wouldn't say nothing else is damaged. Some of these files go back decades. Who knows what the lunatic was after?"

Pradock moaned. "Please don't touch anything."

Poor guy. But his methods wouldn't solve this case. A supernatural case called for a supernatural solution. While Pradock moved to the new evidence, Flores nodded at me to proceed.

I wasn't used to doing this with an audience that had no idea what I did, but it looked like I wasn't going to be left alone in here, not if Reese had anything to say about it. With a very thin rubber glove slipped over one hand, I surreptitiously hovered over the desk. The impression was so obvious it almost glowed like a cancer cell. This would not be fun.

By binding up my fear of the pain, my anger at the murderer, and my doubt in my uncle into a solid, woven wall around my own physical well-being, I touched the spot with my gloved hand. Even through the leather and with all of my wards at full strength, the agony of the victim ripped through my feet until I staggered and almost fell into the body.

Collins squinted at me, but he didn't say anything. The disdain that vibrated from him registered as nothing more than background noise. Still, I couldn't let his ignorance sway me.

I didn't know this lawyer and had no idea if he was a good person or not. But I did know that no one deserved to die like that. If I could aid in any way to catch this fire starter and make sure no one else died at his hands, then I could tolerate the memory of pain. After taking a deep breath and recentering myself—this time truly prepared—I touched the spot again.

The agony of melted feet assaulted me again, but I pushed it aside as if deflecting a dodgeball to the back of the court. Leaned against the desk because his feet would no longer hold his weight, Grayson screamed.

The same voice from the park and from the front desk spoke. "The guard's unconscious. There's no one else here to scream for. And I thought lawyers were supposed to be smart."

A metal drawer slammed shut, and I realized the fake delivery man was behind Grayson. *Please come where I can see you,* I begged the memory to be useful. I was not a martyr and didn't believe that me experiencing this poor man's agony would lessen it in anyway.

The delivery man moved back to the front of the desk. Before I celebrated, he was little more than a brown blur because the victim's eyes were so full of tears. Dammit!

"Look. This will all end if you simply tell me which cabinet to look in. It's an Orem Cranston case right about the same time he died."

Grayson swallowed, and I swore he tasted his own flesh just from the smoke in the air. Oh god, there were new nightmares in my future. "It's not . . . It's not in alphabetical order. There's a guide in the top drawer." He patted the desk as best as he could without tumbling to the ground.

The delivery man pulled his hat off and put it back on. "Well, you should have said that to begin with. All that confidential stuff just made you lose your feet."

"Please, please let me go," begged Grayson. He blinked rapidly and the delivery man came into focus as he moved closer to the desk.

I recognized him immediately as Arnold Shortman, the intern from Amelia's work.

Those cold eyes and that youthful face looked cheerful as it pulled a huge binder from the desk. "Ah, here it is. I don't need you anymore."

"No, please!" yelled Grayson.

With the answers I needed, I yanked my hand from the desk. "Flores," I said, probably a bit too loudly as I stumbled backward to lean against the wall.

He rushed to my side, hands hovering, not knowing if he should touch me or not. "What did you see?"

"I know who it is."

Chapter Twenty-One

Reese cursed from between file cabinets. "Are you
fucking kidding me? I assumed the mess I saw from
the doorway involved files from our case strewn about
during the struggle. But these are old cases from—"

I interrupted her, "Orem Cranston's time."

Flores, Collins, and Reese all stared at me. After experiencing the torture of the victim, all I wanted was to curl up with
a bottle of tequila for numbness and Tucker for comfort.

I didn't have the energy to make excuses for how I knew
what I did, so I spoke to Flores only. "Arnold Shortman did this.
He's an intern at Stratagem so he's connected to at least two of
these. He was super angry at the programmer Udelhoven." The
unique anger signature was just like the impression on the rock.
"I bet if you get his info from Amelia, you can connect him to
Ginger Chan as well. But I have no idea why he'd want the files
from Orem Cranston."

Not one to be left out, Reese held up the ledger Arnold
pulled from the desk drawer in the impression. "A cursory
inspection shows a file missing from a Hayward family."

"Hayward?" I leaned harder against the back wall. "That's
Emblyn and Emmett's last name. Their parents died in a fire."

Reese's instincts must have caught up, though all I felt was a touch of anger. She might have exuded more but the fresh impression had taken a toll on my abilities. "All of these fire deaths can't be a coincidence. What about Liam Anderson?"

Maggie's story immediately popped up. She thought they'd caught the wrong person. And now a lawyer brought up the name without any prompting. "Is that the victim in your case, the one Grayson Michaels was here working on?"

Though she seemed skeptical, her curiosity must have one out, because she probed how I knew. "He is."

Dammit. It really was all connected. And I could have stopped Arnold as soon as I'd met him. I knew there was something off about him. Was this one more thing I had to feel guilty about? I turned to Flores. "Liam Anderson is the child psychiatrist that died in the same way. That's what I was calling you about when you told me about this. I'll get Amelia to send me Arnold's info." And have everyone get out of that office, just in case the nut job was heading that way next. Whatever his motives, he'd obviously been focused on the foster system and Stratagem had information about many of them. "Oh, and she can pick up Maggie. She'll be able to identify Arnold as the patient who set fires in the lobby of Dr. Anderson's office."

Still full of questions, Flores focused on Reese and the folder in her hand. "We had Orem Cranston listed as a defense lawyer for some of the richest clients. Why would he have a file for two orphans?"

Her emotions switched faster than the TV when the remote was stepped on. "Orem was one of the best. Learned everything I knew from him, not my father." Reese leaned against a file cabinet. I knew exactly how she felt. "Look, I can't give you details without a warrant—frankly I don't know anything about this case anyway—but I can share that Orem spent his last year of life fighting for families pro bono, mostly with the For Anna Agency."

Oh shit. Did Bertram have Orem killed because he was too

desperate to protect the Ems and didn't want anyone else to get custody? Or did someone kill Orem to thwart Bertram from getting custody? Well, they failed so what was the point of any of this? If it was all Bertram, why would he frame an innocent man? One thing was for certain, I wasn't going to solve this mystery or prevent anyone else from getting killed if I didn't tell Flores everything.

My phone dinged telling me Amelia had received my text and she'd meet me downtown with Arnold's info and Maggie. Before I replied to her, just in case I needed to ask her to bring bail money on her way, I confessed the last bit I'd withheld to Flores. "I know who the man in the diner reflection is."

Flores turned so slowly to face me, I wondered if something happened to time.

I could tell him I wasn't sure until just now. I could spurt out my fears for my family and the orphaned ten year olds. I could beat around the bush and blubber until it all finally spilled. Or I could just say it, which was what I chose. "It's Bertram."

Some sort of deity must have been on my side as the anger built inside Flores because Collins got a call. "Hey, Flores, Willis has been brought in, and his lawyer says if we're not there in the next fifteen minutes, they're leaving."

After taking an elongated breath, Flores turned to the staring faces of the rest of the people in the room. "Pradock, let me know if you find anything on those files to identify the perp. Reese, thank you for your help, but please step outside so crime scene can finish their work. Collins, I'll forward you the information I get so you can issue an APB for Arnold Shortman." Without looking at me, he simply waved me to the door. "And you're with me."

Like an admonished child, well aware that I was in the wrong, I kept my head down and simply obeyed. In the elevator, I texted Amelia to meet me at 1200 Travis instead.

Chapter Twenty-Two

The viewing room from the other side of the two-way mirror was much colder than I remembered. Rubbing my upper arms didn't seem to help. I knew better than to go into a building in Houston in July without a sweater, but everything had happened so quickly, I didn't have time to think anything through.

Willis sat at the interrogation table, his knees bouncing and his hands drumming. He wasn't under arrest, so no handcuffs. He was probably reviewing whatever nefarious activity he'd been up to lately, wondering which one he had to lie about today. What would his reaction be when he found out it was a case from almost a decade ago? His lawyer, Robert Chambers, wore shoes and a suit much too expensive for a public defender. *How did Willis afford his fees?* It made me think of the mob movies Forrest always made me watch. Like Willis was part of a bigger organization that took care of legal issues for him.

I wondered how close to the truth that was. With Bertram involved, money wasn't the limiting factor.

My nerves were so frayed, I was relieved I didn't have to be in there reading him. Flores knew all the details to this one. He just needed Willis to confess so they'd have something to present at the retrial. I was certain Flores was keeping me here until he had a chance to put me in that same chair to ask about Bertram.

When Flores opened the viewing room, I didn't do a very good job at suppressing my surprise. "What are you doing in here?"

Before he could answer, a detective I didn't know opened the interrogation room. This wasn't Willis's first rodeo. As soon as the suit entered, he leaned back in his chair and calmed his fidgeting, looking every bit like a man sipping a beer at a bar without a care in the world. I couldn't believe Flores wasn't in there tearing down his every lie.

Flores explained, "If we're taking whatever we get here to trial, it needs to be kosher. That means a relative can't do the questioning."

My body warmed with my fear, while my throat tightened with Flores's anxiety. Instead of piling on, I simply nodded my head in acceptance.

"I'm Detective Harold Grimes." He sat in the chair and leaned back, imitating Willis's stance to a T. Just two guys sharing a beer. No authority dynamic at all.

Until the lawyer busted the mood. "I'm Mr. Ponce's lawyer, Robert Chambers."

Grimes pushed aside the formality, trying to maintain the friendly vibes. "Willis hasn't been charged with a crime. We just have a few questions to ask about an incident that happened eight years ago. Really, you being here is just a courtesy." The detective dismissed the lawyer and addressed Willis again. "I'm sorry we had to drag you in here, but the fact that you were willing to come makes me feel like we'll be in and out pretty quickly."

His style was so much different than Flores's or Collins's. I found myself wrapped up in the drama of it all.

Willis shrugged. "No problem, man. Whatcha got for me?"

"Well, I was wondering how good your memory was. Because we found some new witnesses from an old case and were just wondering if you could help clear up some confusion." His deep voice somehow felt light and friendly.

"Hey, man. Whatever I can do to help."

Detective Grimes dropped a tablet on the table and opened it to a picture I couldn't make out from the other room. "Do you recognize this diner?"

The blood drained from Willis's face, but his expression didn't change. "Nah, man. That doesn't look like my side of town."

Grimes scratched his chin. "Well, that's interesting, because we have a witness that places you there at the same time another crime happened nearby. We're not saying you were involved, because we caught the guy. Would you believe he swears he's innocent?"

"Doesn't everybody?" Willis left out the "man." The questioning must have been hitting close to home.

"Well, here's the thing. There was another guy spotted with you, an older gentleman. We were wondering what information you had about him." Interesting tactic. Grimes chose to ignore Pedro and move right into who Willis was with. That both added evidence the witness was a real one and took pressure off of Willis as the perpetrator.

The lawyer bent toward Willis and whispered something in his ear, but Willis waved him off. He must have thought he had it under control because he kept talking.

"Oh yeah, I remember, man. I went there once to talk to an old guy who said he had a job for me. But nothing came out of it."

"Nothing came of it?" With his arms crossed over his chest and his head down, Flores's fingers tapped his elbows as he listened. I knew he wanted to get in there and wring Willis's neck for what he did to Pedro. The discipline he used to remain not only out of the room, but calm, should be taught. I wondered if I could learn such control like I picked up other empathic abilities.

Grimes leaned forward. "Yeah, job interviews at night can be such a letdown." Before Willis unscrunched his eyebrows in defense, Grimes continued, "So what did this guy look like?"

Willis leaned back again, but this time crossed his arms over his chest. "I don't know, man. Like an old white dude with a full head of graying hair and like eyes and a nose and stuff."

"Yeah, they all look alike, don't they?"

I was really starting to enjoy Grimes's satire. He somehow talked down to the suspect without ever making the guy feel talked down to. Amelia and Grimes would make a good team.

Robert Chambers, however, was not a fan. "Mr. Ponce has said he doesn't remember the man who tried to hire him. So there will be no further questions?" He even scooted his chair back like it was time to go.

Seriously? My arm ached where my fingernails dug into it. I supposed there was a reason this petty criminal continued to be free and Pedro was locked up. The man was slippery. If he felt one bit of the guilt I did, he would pour out everything that happened just to get it off his chest.

Grimes held up an iPad to Willis, ignoring the standing lawyer. "Do you think you could identify him from this line up?

"Line up?" I asked Flores.

He was still angry, but at least it wasn't presently aimed at me. "I threw together a quick line up including your uncle."

Willis's eyes bulged before his lawyer squeezed his shoulder. That silent signal had Willis swallowing hard and attempting a return to his nonplussed attitude. "Nah, man. It was a long time ago. I don't remember him at all."

How did he do that? Brush off the truth so casually? Grimes would never get him to confess. Flores must have come to the same conclusion because he folded himself into the armchair in the back of the room and held his head in his hands. Witnessing his vulnerability stoked a deep anger inside me. Why could I help complete strangers find closure with cold cases, but couldn't help someone I cared about? So many things were out of my control: my uncle hiring a killer, mysterious fires consuming victims, secrets about myself that would implode my relationship with Tucker. I could read emotions, experience strong memories, heal illness, and drain life energy. How could all of these things be so useless?

Wait. I had all of these abilities. And I'd only started with one. What if I'd picked up others over the years? I mean if Enrique could raise people's lust or anger or happiness, could I raise someone's guilt? I'd been present when Enrique performed his unique trick multiple times, enough to learn to resist it. Maybe, just maybe.

As Willis stood and his lawyer opened the door to the interrogation room, I pulled up those old feelings. It was much easier than it should have been. I thought of Sylvia Remington and how she died because I lied to her. The image of her daughter who lost the chance to reconcile with her mother floated in right behind. Acid climbed up from my stomach, but now that I'd started, I couldn't seem to stop. The secrets I kept from my best friends for years and the disrespect I'd shown my brother by calling him Sparrow haunted me. They never went away; I'd just buried them deep so I could function. Finally, the fact that I withheld vital information from the man who had done nothing but trust me and support me. It took every bit of my determination to not slide down the door and cry on the floor.

Before I second guessed myself, I rushed into the hallway and rammed directly into Willis. When he grabbed me with both hands to stop us from tumbling to the ground, I opened up the dam and poured all of my pent-up guilt into him.

Oh my god, did it feel good. Forget yoga or even alcohol. This was the way to deal with pain, hoist it onto someone else. Holy shit, what did I have to feel guilty about? I was a goddess who never made a mistake.

Willis, however, was quite human. He pushed me off of him, and I slammed into the wall but felt no pain beyond heartburn that came back full force. But this time it emanated from Willis.

He wiped a tear from his face and shook his head. "I'm out, man. I had nothing to do with nothing, and I don't know nothing."

He stormed down the hallway. Robert Chambers scrambled to catch up.

Flores popped at the threshold before the door had finished swinging. "I'm assuming that didn't go as planned."

He was talking to me, but Grimes lifted his arms in a full body shrug. "Yeah, not like I planned at all."

Flores stood back as Grimes stalked out. "So where does that leave us?" Flores asked me.

The guilt I pushed off on Willis was truly just a reflection because all of my past incidences crawled up my esophagus and promised to torture me for an indeterminant amount of time. Maybe I did still need that alcohol. "At the bar?"

He held the door open for me as I slunk out.

"You're buying," he said. "And talking."

I wasn't about to argue. I didn't need more guilt.

Chapter Twenty-Three

Sweat still poured down my back as I sat beside Flores on a stool over the marble bar at Treebeards. The block and a half walk in July could've been worse—it could've been storming—but it couldn't have been hotter. Both of us stared at the trio plate we'd ordered while I sipped on my blackberry ginger margarita and Flores nursed his IPA. The black-eyed peas, squash casserole, and dirty rice were more to make us feel like we weren't simply day drinking.

We were totally day drinking.

Flores sighed heavily. "So what happened back there?"

Of course he wouldn't wait for me to answer. I might never decide to do so. I still wasn't sure if what I'd done was kosher or not. If it had worked . . . "I tried something new."

Flores took a long sip of beer, which gave me the opportunity to down my drink and wave at the bartender for another. I was too tired to block Flores's disappointment. I needed the help of my crutch right now. Amelia would be here at any minute anyway. I could pick up my car later.

But Flores wasn't going to let me get away so easily. "And trying something new sounded like a good idea at this juncture."

Oh shit, here came his anger. Luckily, the bartender was

quick, and I had my fresh drink in my hands ready to medicate. "Grimes wasn't getting anywhere. And . . . And it's Bertram. I thought I'd left my family behind, but they keep coming back and not in a friendly reunion kind of a way."

"Family, huh?" Flores pushed his drink away as I just about inhaled my second margarita. "You mean, like a cousin who's in prison for a crime he didn't commit. You mean, when we have a witness who knows what really happened in our clutches under the best interrogator I've ever seen, and then . . . What happened exactly?"

"Yeah, well, maybe you shouldn't have trusted me with something so important when I'm just as emotionally compromised as you are!"

My gut clenched with Flores's anger. "Shouldn't have trusted you?"

At that moment, Detective Collins dropped a folder on the bar and placed a hand on each of our stools. "Trouble in paradise?"

Neither of us had noticed him enter the restaurant. Flores scowled and drained the rest of his beer. With a frantic wave at the bartender, I ordered him another one and a shot of tequila for me. The margaritas weren't going to cut it. Collins's amusement tickled my toes, a disconcerting contrast to Flores's anger clenching my gut. It all needed to be shut down.

Collins's smug look didn't help matters. "What? No drink for me."

Flores and I didn't make eye contact, but he did have the bartender bring out a Miller Lite for Collins while we sat there awkwardly, and Collins hovered between us like a child waiting for his parents' acknowledgement.

Which wasn't that far from the truth. "So is no one going to ask me about the folder?" Collins took a sip of his cold beer with his eyebrows raised.

Somehow, his teasing helped Flores calm down. "Tell me it's something useful for Pedro's case."

Collins scooted between us to set down his beer and grab some silverware. "That's not how evidence gathering works. You get whatever you find whether it's useful or not." Around a big bite of dirty rice, he continued, "That is unless you put me on the trail."

He flipped open the folder in front of Flores, who quickly moved his beer before the paper rubbed off the condensation on his glass. Collins pointed to lines I strained to see around his bulk. "If you'll notice, Pedro's lawyer was court appointed with a ton of school debt and more pressing financial issues. Now he's a wealthy landlord with properties all over the state."

Flores's anger had dampened, but so had my empathy. The alcohol helped with that, but it sure numbed my reasoning, because I couldn't see how that made any difference. "It's been eight years. Is that unheard of for a lawyer to change careers and get rich?"

Collins didn't look at me, so I ordered another shot and sat back with my arms crossed. He did continue explaining to Flores though. "His stars changed right after Pedro's case, and I couldn't track the money. Then I found this loan he got from his sister, the high school chemistry teacher, for a million dollars."

Now I was paying attention. "Like *Breaking Bad?* Was it drugs?"

Flores's lip tilted up. Was that almost a smile? Could he maybe forgive me.

Collins, however, was not amused. He obviously liked being the star and resented me pushing in on his big moment. "Luckily it's not drugs. Otherwise, none of this would be relevant." He flipped to the next page in the folder. "As you can see here, his sister was gifted a two million dollar house by a foundation called the For Anna Agency, who not only helps foster kids find permanent homes, but also rewards teachers who go above and beyond for their students. Well, they rewarded one teacher one time anyway."

Flores said, "For Anna Agency was the one Ginger Chan worked for."

Lightbulbs were going off all over the place as Collins added, "Dr. Liam Anderson was on the board at the For Anna Agency, at least in the paperwork."

Flores seemed to catch on to where Collins was going. "Is it a legit corporation?"

"Well." Collins took another bite of dirty rice, which made me dive in for a bite of the squash. Not bad. Salty, savory, a bit mushy, but in the best way. Shit Collins was still talking. Maybe I should lay off the alcohol during the revelation part. "The lawyer's sister sold the house a year later and split the money with her brother, I mean, they made some sort of trust, but anyway, the For Anna Agency is one of many shell companies for Portal Energies."

The squash casserole stuck in my throat, and I hacked until I could breathe again.

Flores would normally look concerned, instead he turned an annoyed eye at me. Would Tucker ever look at me like that? I waved my hand to tell Flores I was all right, to stop Collins from continuing, and to wipe the Tucker thought from my brain.

With both men staring at me, I caught my breath and took a drink of my untouched water. "Portal Energies is my uncle's company."

Collins whistled. "You have one fucked-up family, Fauna."

"That's no secret." Time to confront Bertram. If we couldn't get anything out of Willis, maybe I could convince my uncle to fess up. There was no doubt he was involved in the death of Orem Cranston. What we didn't know was why?

When I looked back at Flores, his face had lightened in relief. "Corrupt lawyer. He was bribed to lose the case. Had to have been."

I added, "And we should be able to connect Arnold with Bertram."

His smile made my heart melt, even as my entire body tingled with his stoked hope. "We can get Pedro a re-trial now."

Collins set his beer on the counter a bit heavily. "Who's the hero now?"

"I owe you, my friend." His face back to business, Flores waved for the check. "I'll work on the search warrants for Dr. Liam Anderon's files from the For Anna Agency." He nodded to Collins. "You get the warrant for the arrest of Robert Chambers, so my hands are still clean on that end. If two independent cases we happen to be working on intersect, no judge is going to bat an eye."

"Did you say Dr. Liam Anderson?" Maggie's sweet voice came through just before her curiosity tickled my fingers and tightened my gut.

Right behind her, Amelia's unique blend of protectiveness and worry made me feel safe. "The boys told us y'all were down here."

My throat clenched at everything I had to line up for them. "I'll explain everything."

When the bartender offered the black folder to Flores, I swiped it up. "I said I was paying. You boys go about your paperwork."

Collins headed toward the door, obviously happy to be rid of me for a bit, but Flores hesitated. "Are you sure you're safe? You've been staying at your uncle's, right?"

His concern was adorable but unnecessary. I could take care of myself. "The Ems are over there. If I'm in danger, then so are they. I can't leave them alone."

"Who's in danger now?" Amelia's mood migrated to annoyance.

Before I could explain, Collins busted back in with his phone on his ear. "You're not going to believe this. Grimes says Willis returned in tears and he's confessing to everything against his lawyer's insistence he stop. And I mean everything he's done. He's at"—Collins tilted the phone closer to his ear—"age twelve.

If we hurry back, we'll arrive before he gets to the time of the crime we're actually interested in."

Holy shit. The guilt thing worked. Apparently, I gave him too high a dose. I wondered if it would work on Bertram.

Flores shoved right from his stool and headed toward the door. He seemed to realize I wasn't beside him and looked over his shoulder with a raised eyebrow.

"I'm coming."

"So are we." Amelia's tone didn't leave room for debate, and none of us argued with her.

Chapter Twenty-Four

When we got back to the police station, I was happy for the dullness in my senses. Everyone in there was on high alert with guns drawn pointing at Willis who held a gun to his own head and blubbered on and on about things he'd done in his life. Beside him, but not close enough to make physical contact, Robert Chambers begged his client to put the gun down and shut up.

Oh shit. The guilt trip worked a bit too well. Fuck me. Every time I tried to help with my powers, I somehow made things worse.

Flores held me back when I tried to pass through the glass doors. "No, you stay here." His voice left no room for argument. I didn't really want to get in-between all of those pointed barrels anyway, but I just couldn't leave. Plus, I couldn't put Maggie and Amelia in more danger.

"Maybe you two should just go." The alcohol I'd generously imbibed helped numb the sheer level of panic and anger in the room, but it buzzed along my body like warring entities anyway. I needed to get them out of here before it exploded.

Amelia put Maggie behind her like she was some sort of human shield, but she didn't budge. "I'm not leaving without you." She was still mad at me, and yet she wasn't leaving. I wouldn't push her away. I didn't have the strength to be alone.

With his gun held steady but casual at the same time, Grimes talked to Willis in a soothing manner. But all I could make out was Willis's ranting.

"I didn't mean to shoot the lawyer. It was an accident." Either Willis made it a habit of killing lawyers or he was talking about Orem.

Collins scoffed at his statement. But I knew based on the guilt dragging Willis down so much that I could feel it radiating from him above the fear and anger coming from the collective police presence, Willis wasn't lying.

Flores's voice comforted me, though it didn't seem to do anything for Willis. "If it was an accident, why did you have to bring Pedro in?"

Chambers shouted, making the already tense officers jump. "Don't say a word, Willis!"

Ignoring his lawyer, Willis continued to confess. "No one would've believed me that it was an accident. That pistol had a light trigger or something. It shouldn't have gone off. The client insisted none of it could be tied to him, and Pedro had no contact with him." He closed his eyes and straightened the gun against his temple.

Flores shouted, "Wait!" at the same time the rest of the drawn guns tensed.

I probably should have closed my eyes or walked away or anything but what I did—which was walk straight through the doors and in-between the cops and Willis. Even with dulled senses, it was like pushing through water, the emotional tension was so high in the room. Surely the tequila shots didn't have anything to do with this poor decision making, but they did dull the physical bombs for my empathy.

Flores tried to grab my shoulder with one hand, but Amelia —who had walked in behind me—put a hand on his shoulder. "She can do this."

She had no idea what I was going to do, but her faith in my abilities bolstered my resolution. I caused the problem, now I would end it. I didn't see that I had any other choice. With the obvious weight on Willis's shoulders, nothing the cops said would stop him from ending the pain. This was my fault and only I could fix it. I would not carry the guilt of a man ending his life.

Apparently, my arrival surprised him because Willis looked up and his weapon sagged. "You should leave."

"Not yet. I need to help first." Just like when I pulled health from Michelle after she attacked me, maybe I could siphon off the guilt I amplified in Willis. Somehow Enrique could do this at a distance, but he also never left such a strong impression that stayed around after he left—it kind of followed him like a cloud. Whatever I'd done was totally different. Somehow, I knew I needed to touch Willis. But as soon as he put down the gun, every cop in this place would be on him. So that wasn't the answer either.

Well, my instincts got me into this mess; let's see if they could get me out. "Willis, my name is Fauna, and I think I know what's happening."

"God is punishing me." Tears welled in his eyes at such a volume, I wasn't sure he could see me. "And I deserve it."

"No, Willis. It's not God." I froze for a moment. I couldn't say it was me. "Stop for just a moment and think of when the feeling started. Where were you?"

He blinked. "Outside the interrogation room. You ran into me and . . ." He rubbed his eyes with the back of his free hand and focused on Grimes. "You drugged me!"

A dozen things all happened at once. Flores yelled at me to get down. Willis pointed his gun at Grimes. And I tackled Willis before he could shoot or be shot. Someone grabbed me by the shoulders to get me off and get to Willis. Before whoever it was got a good grip, I plastered my hands on Willis's cheeks. The salty sour smell of tears and sweat assaulted me a second before his guilt hit me like a Mack truck. Using the same pull I had on Michelle, I absorbed Willis's guilt. At least the edge of it, which was all I had time for before I was ripped away from him, and Willis was flipped over on his belly. His gun flew across the floor.

As I tried to reorient myself, the tension in the room busted like a bubble and tore through my psyche. Flores held me upright, which was a good thing, or I would have collapsed on the floor. Even though I'd taken the edge off of Willis's guilt, I didn't feel guilty myself. It was more like being high as if I'd been sprinting and dopamine flooded my brain. I really should run more.

"Fauna, are you okay?" By the time I registered Flores saying my name, there was a tinge of panic lacing his voice. I wondered how many times he'd said it before I heard him.

Amelia wheeled a chair under me. "Did it work? Did you drain him?"

"Drain him?" Collins asked. "I'm not writing this report."

Flores set me down in the chair and kneeled in front of me. "Are you okay?"

My cheeks cracked oh so gently as every inch of my body felt simultaneously numb and super sensitive. "I think so. Just exhausted."

Maggie pointed to a picture of Arnold on Flores's desk. "Why do you have this?"

My hand rubbed Flores's cheek. "Willis confessed. Pedro will be free. Oh, is that a butterfly." Something flew right over Flores's head. Something light and shimmery and my eyes blurred.

The rest of the world started to fade. I thought I heard Amelia say, "I'll take her home," but I wasn't sure of anything anymore. Then I couldn't see, and everything went black.

Chapter Twenty-Five

S till not quite aware of my surroundings, I blinked myself awake. Vague memories of Amelia bringing me home flashed through my mind. I remembered she said she would call Tucker, and I told her not to. I just needed some rest. How would I explain that my illness came from absorbing the emotional trauma of another? I hadn't confessed anything yet. Was it too late?

Before me, near a large staircase were two people arguing. As consciousness threatened to bring me back to reality, the throbbing of Michelle's shadow memory hurt. I had to find a way to banish that thing before it drove me crazy.

As my eyes focused, I realized I wasn't at home. The memory of me telling Amelia to take me to Bertram's flashed through me like lightning. I jumped up from the couch that wasn't mine and would have fallen flat on my face if Bertram hadn't grabbed my arm to steady me. My first instinct was to push him off of me, but I wasn't sure I'd stay on my feet if I had.

"Steady, Fauna. You've been in and out of it for over an hour now." His voice was laced with concern, which produced nothing but a derisive laugh from me.

"If only you'd been that concerned about murdering somebody." My anger strengthened my legs, and I managed to push him away without face planting into the coffee table, even though every step required more thought than normal.

Bertram squared up like he was ready to debate a counterpart at a business meeting. "What are you talking about?"

I didn't have the energy to play games. "Willis Ponce made a full confession just now at the police station. Collins connected Portal Energies to the For Anna Agency to the Willis's lawyer. We know you're involved."

With his arms crossed, he simply shook his head, like I was the one who had disappointed *him*. "I did not hire that man to kill anyone. He said he knew how to break into the building, and I simply needed Orem Cranston to listen to reason."

Desperate to be by the exit, I leaned against the entryway pillar. "Listen to reason? You mean about Emmett and Emblyn, don't you? What did you do, Bertram?"

He collapsed onto the couch I'd just vacated and looked up at the ceiling as if he could see through it to where Emblyn and Emmett must have been. "What I said before about me needing to save them, about their mother wanting them to live with me, it's all true. But they had an aunt who didn't believe any of the paperwork, and she was fighting for custody. At first, I thought she just wanted to get paid, but nothing I offered her was good enough." He looked straight at me, and I wanted to believe him so badly. "Fauna, you have to understand. I didn't only need to protect the twins; I had to protect anyone they'd be around. They'd already burnt down their home while toddlers. Who could say what would happen to anyone else who brought them in?"

He still didn't know the Ems weren't fire starters. "If you didn't mean to kill Orem, then why not turn Willis in and why frame another man for the murder?"

My uncle, the man I hoped would be the apex of our new family, continued confessing the horrible things he'd done to get the Ems. I felt in my pockets for my phone to record it, but they were empty. "I couldn't have HPD trace the murder to me, and Willis and I had an electronic trail that could be followed if any of the detectives were determined enough to trace it. Willis said he had someone that would be a perfect patsy. Look, I'm not proud of what I did, but the ends justify the means. Nothing is more important than those twins and you and Heidi."

"What are you talking about?" Feeling protective of the Ems, I moved toward the stairwell. I couldn't feel them with my senses so numb, but with the way Bertram kept looking up at the ceiling, it was a logical guess. I wasn't helpless after all—as long as I had any energy left to fight with.

Bertram rubbed his face. "There's so much you should know, so much your father should have taught you. But he'd already broken so many of our laws, he was beyond reason."

"Our laws? What are you talking about?" In the recess under the stairwell, my senses were overwhelmed with the same familiar impression left all over town a few months ago, the same one that sat in the corner of my bedroom interrupting my sleep. I remembered the strong feeling of it when I first woke up. "Shit, Bertram. Michelle was here."

He stood up and put his hands in his pocket. "I know, Fauna. I invited her."

"Can I come out now? I want to play." Michelle, who had somehow found time between running from the police and apparently conspiring with my uncle to dye her hair blue again, stepped into view at the top of the stairs. My heart dropped as she drug Emblyn and Emmett out of the shadows by the scruff of their necks. "What kind of babysitter doesn't get to play games with the kids?"

"A sadistic one," I answered. To the Ems, I asked, "Are you hurt?"

They simultaneously shook their heads, though the fear in their eyes showed there were more kinds of damage than physical.

Michelle wasn't done taunting me. "If you get close to me, I'll send these two into a coma so deep you won't be able to revive them for years."

Bertram sighed. "Now, Michelle, you know that's not acceptable."

"What are you yelling at me for, Bertie? I'm following orders. She's the rogue one."

Even with everything that happened, Michelle was still somehow jealous of me. My chest hollowed and my abdomen tightened as her strong emotion intensified while she walked down the stairs, basically dragging the children.

"Wait. How am I the rogue one? I've never killed anyone."

Michelle curled her lip up. "I'm tasked with protecting the mission, which sometimes means getting your hand dirty, princess."

Emblyn whined as Michelle gripped her neck tighter. My anger rose, and I started doing the math. If I could get her to let go of the children, then I could drain her again and use that energy to get us out of here.

Bertram shook his head at Michelle. "That's enough. It's not Fauna's fault she doesn't know all the details." He moved around the furniture to be closer to the stairwell.

I backed away as Michelle squeezed the kids tighter near the bottom. She loosened her grip slightly, but the kids looked so scared, I knew I had to deescalate this somehow.

With my hands up, I surrendered. "Okay, fine, I give up. Tell me what my father was supposed to."

He pulled a wheeled carry-on bag from the closet and moved to the Ems. I tried not to flinch as he approached them. I don't know why I felt so protective, but that instinct was strong at the moment. I couldn't imagine what parents went through.

"Emblyn, Emmett, I need you two to pack up some clothes, toiletries, and one thing you can't live without. Don't worry about what you miss. We'll buy new stuff once we get settled."

Neither of them reached for the bag; they kind of shook and simultaneously looked at Michelle.

Bertram sighed like the weight of the world rested on his shoulders. "Michelle, you're going to have to let go of them."

Her blue hair shimmered under the lights as she shook her head no. "I'm not letting them go with her here looking at me like that."

If anything, my expression darkened. As soon as she released them, I was definitely going to . . . *Stop it, Fauna,* I told myself. *You're supposed to be deescalating. Save the fight for when you're at your strongest. As long as we stayed together, nothing would happen to those kids.*

Instead I said, "I want everyone safe. I won't do anything until I get an explanation." To myself, I added, *But after that . . .*

Bertram said, "You see, Fauna is being completely reasonable. Your turn."

Michelle's scowl deepened, but she released the Ems. "Fine."

Emmett took the suitcase, but neither of them moved until I nodded, then they shot up the stairs.

Bertram raised an eyebrow at me. He'd apparently caught the exchange. For a moment, I wasn't sure anything got past him. "Grab, your cousin's bag while you're up there," he shouted up to the children. "She's coming with us."

When he said it out loud, I knew he was right. I wasn't about to let him take those kids without me. "So tell me, Bertram. Why do you need us? What did my father fail to tell me?"

Watching Bertram work, I knew where Forrest got his con artist talent from. It wasn't from Mom's side of the family. "There's so much to tell you. Let us get somewhere safe, and I'll tell you everything." He left Michelle and I glaring at each other while he moved to the back of the hallway and into his formal office.

She needed to answer some things for me as well. "How long have you been working for Bertram?"

After laughing so hard she bent over and slapped her knees, Michelle wiped tears from her eyes. "Since always, you moron. I might not have one of the abilities he's collecting, but he couldn't do any of this without me. I'm vital."

"Shit, Michelle." I guess she hadn't been obsessed with my brother like I'd always believed. "Bertram is just using you. Can't you see that?"

"That's all anyone ever does. At least this way, I'm an important part of what's to come." Michelle leaned against the railing and yelled up, "Hurry up, rugrats! We need to get out of here before Fauna's cop friends come to check on her."

That reminded me I had to message Flores somehow. A recheck of my pockets verified I didn't have my phone. I always had my phone. Where could it have gone?

"Looking for this?" Michelle held up my lifeline. "Forrest told me about that 911 trick you pulled to free yourself from that serial killer. I'm good at my job, and Bertram *does* need me."

"I certainly do," Bertram interrupted our argument with passports in his hand. He opened one up and then handed it to me.

"How did you get my passport? Wait. I don't have a passport." I flipped open the thick blue cover to see my picture, a recent one too, but everything else was made up. "Do I look like a Toni Wilde?"

"Yes," Bertram and Michelle said at the same time.

Bertram handed Michelle a passport and tucked five others in his jacket pocket.

This was no time to leave anything unasked, "Why so many fake passports?"

He looked up as the Ems stomped down the stairs, the full suitcase banging behind them. "We're heading to Arkansas to pick up your brother and Heidi first. Once you know everything, you'll understand."

"What about Sparrow?" I didn't know why I thought of my ungifted brother, but he was a part of this family too. He should be involved, right?

Bertram took the suitcases from the kids and handed them

to Michelle who didn't look happy about her downgrade to luggage handler. "He'll be fine. Since he has no empathic abilities, he can't help us right now. He'll be safer on his own until after we fulfill our mission. Then we'll bring him on board so he can share in the wealth of power."

I shook my head as I took the hands of the trembling Ems. "That didn't sound villain-y at all. Which side do you think you're on?"

While retrieving another suitcase, I could only guess was his already packed and ready to go, Bertram paused at the closet by the door. "You haven't even met the villain yet. What we're fighting for is going to happen one way or another. The difference will be who is there when it does."

"And you need specific empathic abilities to accomplish whatever these mysterious goals of yours are?"

Bertram's voice sounded strained for the first time all night. Maybe annoying people was my greatest power. "Obviously. Just get in the car and I'll explain while we're on the road." He dismissed me again and turned to Michelle. "You changed the license plates, right?"

"Yes," Michelle was just as exasperated. "I've been doing this running thing for much longer than you. All the times Forrest and I had to scramble to leave town? I could write a book."

As curious as I was with what Bertram was up to, I couldn't leave the children in his care. I bent down and whispered to Emmett and Emblyn while Michelle and Bertram gathered the last bits they needed from the closet. "Do you remember the books you showed me in the *drawer*?" I emphasized the last word with as much suggestion as I could muster.

Emblyn nodded quickly followed by a big smile from Emmett. I took their hands and connected them to each other.

"You know, the Ems and I have different plans," I said which brought Bertram's head out of the closet and Michelle's body closer to his with her characteristic scowl back on her face.

"What are you talking about?" Bertram sounded as exasperated as I did when I begged him for answers he continued to withhold. I would make him tell me when Flores had him in custody.

It was good to have the upper hand again. "If you need certain powers, I'm assuming that means you need fire starters."

While Bertram's mouth opened and closed like a fish out of water, Michelle squinted and dropped the suitcases. "What are you up to?"

She did spend more time with me after all, but I'm guessing she didn't spend any with the Ems. "Emmett and Emblyn can't start fires. But they can do this. Now!"

Chapter Twenty-Six

The air vibrated in the open entryway, as if it had suddenly been pressurized. Bertram barely had time to look surprised before the Ems used their telekinetic ability to shove him and Michelle into the closet and slam the double doors closed. I grabbed the chair by the front door and shoved it under the handles before they burst right back out. Grabbing the keys off the floor, I motioned the frozen Ems forward.

"Come on, Emmett and Emblyn. We're leaving."

My authoritative voice seemed to break through whatever had them frozen. Still holding hands, they gave the vibrating closet doors a wide berth.

On the porch, Emmett looked up to me with tears in his eyes. "Daddy Bertram is so mad."

Emblyn mirrored his terror I was too weak to block. "We should go back."

My stomach cramped so violently, I dropped to my knees. That kind of effect when I still wasn't at my peak showed how strong their combined emotions truly were. Taking both of their chins in my hands, I made them look at me. "You should never be that afraid of someone who loves you. Do you understand?

What Bertram has shown you isn't love. Come with me and I'll keep you safe and we'll work on the other parts."

When Emmett and Emblyn's tone changed to hope, my cramps gave way to a much more pleasant full body tingle. After a quick glance at each other, like they conferred without saying a word, Emblyn spoke for the two, "Okay."

At least they weren't into long speeches. "Let's go!" I shuffled them toward the already running Lexus in the driveway. Michelle wasn't kidding. She really was prepared for quick exits, though I couldn't imagine her and Forrest ever fled a town in something as nice as this. I know we didn't when I traveled with them.

Emmett stopped before he jumped into the back seat. "What about our stuff?"

"Um." Shit I wasn't even sure where we'd go except to 1200 Travis.

Before I came up with an answer, a deep hatred flowed through the air as if it were directed at us. Out of instinct, I grabbed the Ems and dropped to the ground. My hair flew up as a goddamn fire ball flew by and exploded in the trees of the neighbor's yard.

A yell of rage seemed to pierce my brain. "I have you now. And you won't get away again."

Fuck. Who wanted me dead this time? A glance up showed a young man in a brown delivery outfit, much like the one the attacker wore at the law office. Arnold was after *me*? To the Ems, I whispered, "Do either of you have a phone?"

Emblyn pulled a Hello, Kitty! case out of her pocket.

"Good," I said. "When I stand, you two run across the street and call 911."

Emmett shook his head no. But Emblyn nodded with determination, which made Emmett take a deep breath and mirror her nod.

"You've got this." In one swift movement, I stood and took two steps in front of them while they scrambled up from the manicured lawn. "Hold up. You can have me. But these kids have nothing to do with it."

"It's not you I want." When the Ems took off for the street, the deranged Arnold shot another fireball not two feet in front of them.

The heat pushed them backward and they slammed into the Lexus. Their little heads bashing into the metal almost stopped my heart. How can you love something so instantly when you barely know them?

My feet couldn't carry me fast enough to their sides, even as I yelled at the deranged fire starter. "What the fuck is wrong with you? They're just children."

"Well, so was I. But they were the chosen, and I was tossed aside like trash. If they'd never been born, I'd still be with Mom living happily ever after."

Thankfully, Emblyn and Emmett seemed fine, though thoroughly shaken. By some miracle, Emblyn had managed to hold onto her phone. After I got them back to their feet and tried to not think about all of the car explosions I'd seen in my television-viewing life, I stood protectively in front of them. "If I knew what you were talking . . ." Arnold pulled his arm back, and fire pooled in his palm. If I wasn't in imminent danger, it would be fascinating. But hadn't I seen this before? The park! So it's true. He's connected to all of these fires. "It was you who killed Ginger Chan in the soccer park."

He cradled the ball of flame in his hands instead of throwing it. "She wouldn't tell me where they were. I know she helped place them. My aunt said Ginger testified against her when she tried to get custody of the rugrats."

I needed to distract him long enough for Emblyn to call 911. "Aren't you Amelia's intern Arnold Shortman?"

"So you recognize me. My name's not Arnold though, not really. I needed access to all those bleeding-heart companies that protected those brats like they were royalty or something. And they wouldn't let in an intern who'd been locked up for most of my life, thanks to those two!"

He flung the fireball, but his hand shook so hard with anger, that it flew wildly over our heads. At least, he looked like he was willing to talk. If I could keep him going long enough for help to arrive, maybe I could get the Ems out of here safely.

"Just in case you don't remember, I'm Fauna Young, and I'm so sorry for whatever happened to you. I also had a shitty childhood. It's not easy growing up in this world when you're not like everyone else." For the first time, I wished my gifts were a bit more showy so I could make him relate to me more. "My empathy isn't as displayable as your fire starting, but I can literally feel your anger right here in my gut, and it hurts. Let me help you."

"Help me? There is no help for me. When I was little, my abilities were cute and unique and special. Then they were born, and I was a danger and unpredictable."

Holy shit, all of the pieces started to fall into place. "You're their older brother?"

His laugh echoed in the cul-de-sac even as the sound of sirens in the distance alerted us to our limited amount of time before the firetrucks arrived. "Yes, I'm a Hayward, just like those two, regardless of what fancy name has been bestowed on them. I was the first born and should have been the last. My parents paid for their mistake when I burned down the house. I should have stuck around and made sure the little home-wreckers went up too. I won't miss this time."

A new fireball grew in his hand. If I wasn't mistaken, it was much slower to form than the previous ones. Surely he had to weaken just like I did. Though the adrenaline rushing through my system made me feel like a superhero at the moment. If I could get close enough, maybe I'd have enough in me to drain him so he wouldn't have energy to use his power anymore.

"Ethan?" The Ems said at once.

His hand dropped a little, and I stepped two steps closer.

"See, you can hear it too. They're just children. They had no control over what your parents did or didn't do. They're victims just like you."

"When they released me to the care of my aunt and the drugs finally left my system, I thought I was cured, that whatever this anger was inside of me was quenched forever. Then she told me the twins were still alive. My fingertips burned yet again, and I knew at that moment that I had to end them if I was ever to have a life. My aunt told me about the lawyer who tried to get them back, but he had died and no one else would take the case. The only other name she knew was Ginger Chan and the For Anna Agency."

Two more steps closer. "That's why you worked at Amelia's. You needed access to their records."

He bounced the fire in his palm like it was a tennis ball. "Turns out, children advocacy groups don't like to hire newly released adults with sealed juvenile records. They wouldn't even take me as a volunteer. I had to find another way to access their records. I didn't have much to do while locked away except learn a skill. Computers do what you tell them to. It worked for me."

"Now that I understand. I own a computer store myself. And I'm not a stranger to the foster care system. It's why both members of my staff are former foster children. If you're as good as you say you are, maybe we could work something out?" You know, that was if I could get him to be less murdery. Time to make a leap, I hoped Emblyn was on the call with 911 and they were picking all of this up. "What happened with the programmer?"

Ethan seemed quite willing to just dump everything on the lawn. For a moment I felt sorry for him. He had to be so lonely. That was a state of mind I could relate to. Then horrible things poured out of his mouth again. "Matthew? That arrogant jerk found out I'd been snooping in his files. I couldn't let him spill the tea before I'd finished."

Just then Bertram burst through the door of his house.

Chapter Twenty-Seven

I didn't know how Bertram freed himself from the closet. I couldn't see Michelle, though I could definitely sense her. Before I could signal for some sort of cooperation for tackling the crazy man with the fire, he provided one for me. Ethan threw the fireball he'd been forming to the porch. It exploded instantly setting the house on fire.

Bertram was pretty spry for an old man and leaped out of the way. Michelle's impression faded in the overwhelming extreme heat. As much as I didn't wish her well, I also didn't want to see her dead.

Now was my moment. I sprinted the last few steps and tackled the scrawny boy. As soon as we hit the ground and our skin touched, his anger soaked into my very being. An animal roar ripped out of me, and for a moment, I felt like I floated above my body and watched what was going on. My hands gripped his throat out of instinct instead of volition. Before I gave in to the fury that felt so good, I focused on sapping his energy.

He whined like the child he really was. "What are you doing? Get off me." His palm flashed red as if he tried to form more fire.

With my hands still tight around his neck, I tapped into my healing ability. The boy glowed in an entirely different shade of gold than I'd seen with anyone else. It wasn't an illness, unless this was what madness looked like. With no time to analyze what I was seeing, I pulled on the light, just like I had with Michelle, just as I'd accidentally done with Amelia. Remembering how out of hand it all got the one time I'd done this, I swallowed Ethan's fury, stamped it down to live in my gut where it belonged instead of taking over my entire being. My hands loosened around his throat, but I didn't release my grip, unwilling to lose the contact with his skin.

His energy felt hot just like his skin under my palms. It burned my insides while refueling my drained empathic abilities. And his anger weakened at the same pace as his energy in general. His palm stopped glowing and tears fell from his eyes as I felt sadness overwhelm the fury.

As good as it felt to absorb the energy I desperately needed, I started to feel like a vampire. I didn't like that image at all, so I stopped the flow. Though I didn't let him up yet, I did remove my hands from his throat to his shoulders that felt unnaturally cold.

He pulled up a fist and shook it. "Come on. Why isn't it working?"

Since my empathy was fully charged again, I could feel his anger morph to sadness then hopelessness. Before his skip through emotions ended it all for me, I rolled off him and stared up into the dark sky highlighted with orange all around me where small fires grew. Ethan rolled to his side and beat his head with his fists. Inside, a bigger fire grew as Ethan regained energy much faster than I ever did. That anger of his was irrepressible it seemed.

I rose to my knees and bent over him. "Ethan, stop it right now. Or I'll take more."

His anger morphed to sadness. I was so sensitive to any change that my eyes welled up with tears. "I've been able to do this"—a tiny flame popped up on his extended finger—"since I was two. Mom thought it was cute. Sometimes, I had a bit of a temper, I'll admit. But I'd never hurt anyone. We were fine. When I was eleven, those brats were born, and she got scared I'd hurt them. Everything changed, and she sent me away. The whole world was out to get me. No one but her believed I was doing this on my own; they assumed I was getting ahold of matches somehow."

I looked at the flames spreading fast inside the beautiful home. "Sure. Matches." I remembered how ridiculous what I could do seemed to the mundane world. It didn't take long for you to quit telling people.

Bertram was beside me, covered in dirt and minor scrapes that shown at me almost as brightly as his burning porch. I braced, expecting him to attack the fake intern. Instead, he squatted beside him and helped Ethan sit up. "I believe you. You must be who your mother was contacting me about. She was trying to get you help, Ethan. If I'd known there was another sibling, I'd have taken you in too. What you can do is so rare, you're the first I've found in decades of searching."

Just then the fire trucks arrived, their blaring sirens drowning out any further conversation. Bertram helped Ethan to his feet. "You have to trust me for just a little while and then I'll explain everything."

My body tingled with Ethan's hope. Bertram needed a fire starter. That's why he wanted the Ems to have that ability so badly. He must have been willing to make a deal with a murderer if it meant accomplishing his mysterious goal. He did willingly work with Michelle after all. Maybe even gave her orders to kill. Bertram wasn't the loving caretaker he portrayed in public.

My uncle, who I, apparently, still knew nothing about, motioned me toward Emmett and Emblyn. "Please gather them up before they get lost in the crowd. Telekinesis is also required." While his house burned down and I'd just accused him of murder and conspiracy and he'd almost got blown to pieces by a fireball produced in the hand of a disturbed teenager, Bertram maintained focus on this big scheme of his.

His annoyance at my hesitation twitched my eye. "I will explain everything once we get somewhere safe. You've poisoned them against me so now *you* have to go get them. You're part of this anyway. You're the first."

Just when I was about to explode like Ethan had, Michelle popped up behind Emblyn and Emmett. She grabbed their shoulders so hard, Emblyn dropped her phone and Emmett cried out. A growl rose from deep down inside me, and I pulled my hand back, its palm reflecting the intense heat next to me.

Michelle sneered at me and yelled above the roar of the fire, the whine of the fire engines, and the pulsing in my head. "Are you sure you want to have that fight right now?" Her nod toward the street made me notice movement out of the corner of my eye.

The sidewalk along the cul-de-sac filled with onlookers, some with hoses in their hands. How much had anyone seen? I dropped my hand as quickly as I'd raised it. I didn't know what I'd expected to do anyway. I wasn't a fire starter. I grabbed my head and forced my barriers up. I couldn't keep waffling back and forth between my feelings and those around me. I had to get control back. What I wouldn't do for a shot of tequila right about now. At least the stupid strong emotions built a super strong wall.

By the time I calmed down and realized we needed to get out of there, Emblyn and Emmett had rushed to my side. When their fear only touched my empathy instead of overwhelming it, I sighed in relief. Back in control, it was time to work out an exit plan. "I've got you. Let's get out of here."

The fire engine blocked the Lexus, we couldn't use that to get away if we wanted to. As firemen poured out of their vehicle, some moved to the back to pull out a hose and hook it to the fire hydrant while two others rushed to our lawn. An extremely tall man with shoulders twice as large as his waist waved us away from the flames. "Is there anyone else inside?"

"No," Bertram answered him concisely. "We all made it out safely."

Safely was a bit of a stretch. I wouldn't feel safe until I got the Ems away from Bertram and whatever his evil plan entailed.

The fireman—who had to be half god—guided us through the vehicles parked on the road to the patch of neighbors. "Good. Now get behind the engine and let us handle the fire."

As he jogged off, Michelle cracked her neck. "I'll get us another vehicle."

Bertram indicated our group. "Something big enough with seatbelts for everyone."

"Whoa." I tried to halt the kidnapping. "Emblyn, Emmett, and I aren't going anywhere with you." I almost included Ethan, after all he was just as much a victim of my uncle's as the Ems were. But one look at his hatred still focused on his younger siblings told me it was more than I could handle.

"Dammit, Fauna, can't you just follow directions for—" Bertram would have continued, but the door of one of the cars parked in the curve of the cul-de-sac opened and Willis's lawyer, Robert Chambers, stepped out.

Bertram's face dropped all color, and he moved back from the streetlight with Ethan in tow toward a neighbor's darkened house—they must not have been home since they weren't among the gawkers. Bertram asked the lawyer, "What are you doing here? We're not to be seen together."

The lawyer ignored his secret patron. Instead, he turned to Ethan in an almost robotic manner. "You're the one who killed Dr. Anderson."

The name pulled Ethan from his focus on the Ems. I had no idea why the lawyer was here, but maybe I could get away now, while they were distracted.

Ethan sneered again, as if he thought that was what villains were supposed to do. "That man refused to keep me as a patient.

He said I was beyond his help. He told Mom I needed more than he could offer. That was when they decided to put me on meds that made me loopy. Dr. Anderson"—he spat the *doctor* like it was a dirty word—"was supposed to help me. Just because a few small fires started in his office waiting room. If he didn't make me wait so long, everything would have been fine."

Robert's voice sounded pitiful. It wasn't anything like he'd sounded at 1200 Travis. There was something disconcerting about the tone. "Dr. Anderson was helping me. He was the only one who cared. And you took him from me!" Robert screamed the last sentence and pulled out a gun from his jacket pocket. Before I could register what was happening, he aimed and fired.

Chapter Twenty-Eight

than jerked with the impact. Emblyn and Emmett screamed while the lawyer continued to fire into their brother who had just tried to murder them. The gawking neighbors must have decided it was safer inside their homes that weren't on fire and where no one was shooting people. They scattered quicker than they'd gathered.

Before the deranged lawyer turned his weapon on anyone else, I yanked the arms of the Ems to get them to stop and focus on me. Then I put their fingers together and held their shoulders. "Do it again."

Simultaneously, the two snapped their heads to the lawyer. I felt that swell in the air I'd experienced each time they'd used their telekinetic ability. Then they thrust their hands out and yelled much the way I had when I sapped some of Ethan's strength. The lawyer swiveled his head without stopping his firing, his blue eyes opened wide in shock. Then he flew across the lawn and slammed into his car. The crack of his head sent a shiver down my spine, but I didn't have time to worry about what it meant. Instead, I lunged forward and picked up the gun he'd dropped in his flight.

Out of the dark came Flores. I almost cried in relief.

He took the gun from me and checked the pulse of the shooter all before I could say hello. "Are you all right? I rushed over as soon as I heard the fire call for this neighborhood. I'm so sorry I didn't make sure you were safe."

His calming influence even during this rampage of a disaster was exactly what I needed to refocus. "I'm fine, but Michelle is here somewhere too."

His flash of concern had him grabbing his phone to call for back up. Anxious energy came from the other side of the car. One glance told me the paramedics who had arrived with the firetrucks peeked from behind their vehicle. I pointed them out to Flores while he sent his message. "They want to know if it's clear."

Flores held up the badge around his neck and waved them onto the scene. "Gunman is down, and we have injured."

Right on cue Bertram yelled, "No, no, no, NO!" He'd collapsed next to Ethan, who bled so profusely the thick liquid sat on top of the grass before soaking in. The still flashing lights of the emergency vehicles gave the entire scene a surreal appearance. "I need you. You're essential. You should have come to me immediately. I would have protected you. I knew I should have kept Heidi close."

Was he crying? "Bertram," I said his name gently—something I was certainly not feeling—as I helped him stand and moved him back to make room for the paramedics. My healing ability showed Ethan's insides dim in a way I'd never seen before. Instinctively, I knew it was too late. Even if Heidi had been here, Ethan took too much damage to be saved through our ability. It all made me so sad. And Bertram had orchestrated it all.

Maybe he'd be willing to spill something important while he was in this vulnerable state. "What exactly do you need a fire starter for? Modern technology can easily start fires without any sort of supernatural interference."

My uncle, who looked like an old man for the first time, grabbed my shoulders. "You have a destiny, Fauna. One I would have raised you in, fully aware of, if your father hadn't hidden you so well from me. When I finally tracked him down, your damn mother finished where he started. But you're not the only one required to fulfill our family's destiny. We need to assemble a group of empaths with specific skills. A fire starter is one of them. I thought that was the twins, but it turns out . . ." He trailed off as he watched the paramedics tape up the gunshot wounds in Ethan as best they could to prepare him for transport.

"You still don't get it, do you? These kids need someone to look after them without being a part of some sort of big picture plan which you still haven't explained to me." A sob stuck in my throat when the paramedics dropped what they were doing and started CPR on Ethan.

"Fauna!" Emblyn and Emmett called out for me, and the weak tone in their voice had me push everything aside and run to them.

I got to their sides just as they both collapsed on the ground. "What's wrong?" Asked out of habit more than anything because as soon as I touched them, I saw they were exhausted. Relief washed through me as I pulled them both into my lap. "You're going to be fine. I'll protect you; I promise." I had no idea how, but I knew I would keep that promise as long as I drew breath. I might have failed their brother, but I wouldn't fail them.

With the help of a couple firefighters, the paramedics managed to continue CPR, while transporting Ethan to the ambulance. There was no reason to keep fighting, but how could I tell them that. I was still new to this combo of weird abilities. Hopefully, I was wrong and modern medicine could save him. The poor kid never had a chance in this life. Not with people like my uncle trying to manipulate everything he did.

As one ambulance left, another arrived. Flores waved them over to check out Robert Chambers, who still laid unconscious on the pavement. I probably could have healed him up and let Flores take him in, but I just couldn't seem to work up the energy to use my powers on a man who had just shot a kid in cold blood.

Bertram approached us, the dimming fire that succumbed to the fire hoses flashed in the whites of his eyes. "Come on. Let's get out of here before they ask more questions."

For a moment, I considered going. He was no threat to me and there was obviously so much more I needed to know. But Emmett and Emblyn curled up tighter, hiding their faces in my chest. Mind made up, I held them tighter prepared to fulfill my self-appointed role as their guardian. "We're not going with you, Bertram. Besides, you have more to answer for."

Right on cue, Flores stepped in between us. "Bertram Young, you're under arrest for soliciting the murder of Orem Cranston."

Just when I thought it was all over, Michelle drove a SUV onto the lawn right next to Bertram. She threw open the passenger side door and yelled, "Get in!"

Even though he claimed to be desperate to keep our family together, Bertram didn't hesitate. Apparently, saving his own neck was much more important. He rushed the car and slammed the door closed before Flores took two steps. Flores had his gun out, but I knew he wouldn't fire at an unarmed man.

Yet, it couldn't end this way. Bertram claimed I was the center of something important and I had no idea what that was. If he was in charge, if my father tried to hide us from him, it couldn't be anything good. Still, I had to know. I deserved to know!

Anger took over, and I sprung to my feet. Completely focused on a potted sago palm by the neighbor's mailbox, I used the power I'd sapped from Ethan to manipulate the air around me until I could feel it swirling in a confined area, much like it had with the Ems, and I knew exactly what to do with it. With a twist of my hand, I balled up the pressurized air and pushed it under the pot, then flung it at the side of the stolen SUV. It hit with such force the clay exploded, pushing the SUV's back end into a parked car on the street. That didn't stop Michelle though, as she quickly straightened out the vehicle and punched the gas.

"Oh, no you don't!" I yelled as if she could hear me.

My palms burned, but it felt good. I lifted my hand to see a flame start to grow on top of my skin, but my healing ability vibrated underneath it, preventing the skin from blistering and bubbling. Fear clenched my gut though I felt nothing but fascination. A tug on my pants from both legs had me tilt my head down. Emmett and Emblyn's big eyes starred up at me with that same terrified, vacant look they'd had at the park and when Ethan threw his first fireball.

The flame flickered but held. "I have to protect you."

Flores put a hand on my shoulder that added to my clenched gut. "They're safe, Fauna. You can stand down now."

I'd never experienced his fear before. The shock of it had me drop my hand. The baby fireball faded into the wind like fireflies as it fell harmlessly from my palm.

Pulling on everything I was feeling—confusion, pain, fear, love—I pooled it together and pressed it up into a wall around my mind. I cued my mom's favorite hymn and closed my eyes to concentrate on the soundtrack and the construction until everything was under control again.

When I blinked my eyes back open, Flores tilted my chin to meet his eyes. "Are you all right?"

His fear had faded to worry, and I was easily able to keep it physically separate from my feelings. With one hand on each twin, I snuggled them closer. "I will be." I gestured toward the SUV that had turned the corner and rushed out of sight. "He's gone though. We'll never get Pedro out."

"Bertram doesn't need to be here to free Pedro. Willis made a full confession." Flores's straight to business demeanor helped me maintain my composure. "I'll get Collins out here and more boots on the ground. That vehicle must be one of the neighbors'. He can find which one and get their license plate number so we can put out an APB for the fugitive. Meanwhile," he took a deep breath, "I'm going to need a full statement, while it's fresh."

Considering everything that just went down, I couldn't help but laugh. "Well, I can tell you everything that happened, but I'm not sure you'll want to put it all in the report lest they call psych on both of us."

"Tell me everything and I'll do my best." He stared into the diminishing flames as the efficient HFD took care of them. "It looks like they managed to save both houses."

It didn't matter. "We're not staying here tonight. Can I borrow your phone to call, Sparrow?"

"Hawke." All three of them corrected me.

"Okay, fine, Hawke. He needs to know what's happening and we can stay with him for now."

"I'll assign some uniforms to—"

I interrupted him, "No, you won't. I can take care of myself. And them."

The squeeze I got from the Ems told me they agreed.

"Oh, my head."

Flores spun around with his hand on his holster as I looked over his shoulder. We'd both forgotten about the lawyer who pulled himself up from the ground with one hand, clutching his skull with the other. The paramedics tried to get him to lay still, but Robert pushed them aside.

The obviously confused man slowly rose from the ground and almost fell. As he grabbed the hood of the car his head had bashed into, Robert squinted at the flashing lights of the fire engines. "Where am I?"

Flores pulled out his handcuffs and walked over to the man. "Mr. Chambers, you're under arrest for the shooting of . . ."

"Ethan Hayward." I filled in the blank for him. But before Flores could haul the lawyer away, something about the man's demeanor felt off. I had to get a better look. Once I managed to free myself from the Ems' desperate grip, I put them together and whispered, "Give me just a moment. I'll be right back."

Clutched to each other the way they'd been to me, Emblyn and Emmett both nodded, but their terrified eyes and my clenched gut told me they could run at any provocation. I had to be quick.

"Flores, may I?" I approached the now handcuffed man.

With one hand on the lawyer's elbow, Flores said, "I have to wait for the marked car to pick him up anyway."

Robert blinked at me with his lost brown eyes as I touched his chest. "You're the woman who tackled Willis. Did you bring me here? Was I drugged?"

I had to know if his confusion was due to his hitting his head or something else, something I couldn't quite explain. "What's the last thing you remember?"

Since my powers were recharged and my barriers were up, it was easy for me to read him without getting emotionally invested myself. The sensation of the air on my arms standing straight up along with an itchy scalp verified his confusion but not its source.

As he spoke, I focused on my healing to see what kind of damage he had to his head. "Remember? I was at the police station and my client wouldn't keep his mouth shut."

His skull did glow on one side, but it didn't spread indicating the injury didn't affect his entire brain. Not that I was a medical expert or anything and I'd only had this ability for a few months now, but I didn't think his loss of time was a brain injury thing. And he definitely wasn't lying. I sensed no overt fear or guilt.

Flores's curiosity broke over the mixing emotions of the lawyer, giving my fingers a tickle and my gut a squeeze. All I could offer him was a shrug. There was something here, some familiar shadow that danced around the lawyer, but it could just have been Michelle and that thing she left behind when she went invisible. Studying his deep brown eyes, I couldn't find the truth without a full interrogation.

Before I could express my impressions, a uniformed police

officer arrived with sirens blaring just as the neighbor whose yard we were invading arrived home.

As Flores transported the lawyer to the marked vehicle, four more showed up in quick succession. Policemen poured out of their cars, and Flores quickly took control of the situation getting them to keep the neighbors back and set up a perimeter.

I returned to the children and pulled them into my protective circle and waited for my brother to arrive, wondering what in the world I was going to tell him.

Chapter Twenty-Nine

Flores and I waited on his front porch for the last guests to arrive. It was a momentous day, but I was having trouble concentrating. I still couldn't decide if this was the right thing for the Ems, for me, for Flores. The anxiety from Flores lent evidence to his same doubt—or he was scared something would fall through.

We'd know soon enough. For now, I could distract him. "How's Pedro doing?"

Flores stopped pacing and smiled at me. "I've never seen him happier. Though they won't just let him out. But he has been granted a new trial, and it's looking promising with Willis's full confession and the evidence we found implicating your uncle. I'm sure he'll be found innocent this time if the DA decides to go forward with a new trial at all."

"Really? That would be awesome."

Flores rubbed his sweaty hands on his shorts. Good thing Austin was in the backyard with Tori finishing up the food and decorations. "I think he would have dropped the case immediately if he hadn't just let Reese's client go. He doesn't want to look weak on crime before his re-election next year."

"The news reports about Michelle's escape haven't been kind to his office for sure. Or yours for that matter. Any leads yet?"

"Nothing. How are Forrest and Heidi?"

His concern for my family warmed my heart. "Heidi's wrapping up her reversal of the Wasting Sickness victims in Arkansas. Then they'll head back to Houston to figure out what's happening with this family drama. No sign of Bertram or Michelle. I can't believe Michelle had been working for Bertram that whole time."

"Seems there's a lot about that man left to uncover." Flores simply shook his head. "With his resources, I'm not sure we'll find him unless he wants to be found."

"He said he has plans for me and the other empaths. He'll be back." And Michelle will be with him.

Flores frowned. "If he wants to get to Emblyn, Emmett, or anyone else I care about"—a quick glance at me communicated what he meant by that—"he'll have to go through me first."

"All right macho man, the kids can use your protection. But I assure you, I can take care of myself." I'd always been independent, but in an *I'll hide at work and in my house and no one can hurt me* kind of way. After everything I'd been through recently and with the additional abilities I'd picked up, I truly believed I could handle myself with anything. I'd dealt with the lawyer, hadn't I? Which reminded me. "Has Robert Chambers remembered anything about the shooting?"

"Not a thing. And Collins can't find a connection between him and the psychiatrist. We can't find any motivation for him to seek vengeance for his death. But the lawyer also tried to say he didn't know Bertram, and we know that's a lie." He looked up at me with his head still facing down. "Maybe I can get you in to talk to him."

"Put me in, coach."

Our conversation halted as a shiny BMW pulled into Flores's already crowded driveway. Tucker exited the passenger side seconds before his nephew and nieces squealed out of the back seat.

"Hey, hey, hey, be careful. That's no way to act at a friend's house." Tucker was the best uncle ever. And the way he slipped right into my extended family sent chills down my spine.

Reese Wickman stepped out of the driver's side, expensive leather bag already in hand. She looked like some sort of stunt double to me in her tight jeans and square-necked, cinched-waist blouse. I'd never seen her in anything but a business suit, jacket and all. She walked right up to the bottom of the stairs. "Are we ready?"

"Yes, ma'am," Flores opened the door for her, and they all went inside, except Tucker and me.

He leaned against a column on the porch, and I had to resist setting up my phone to take a TikTok video. The internet would melt, much like I was. "Come here," he said.

And I did. Our love mingled, and I opened a slight gap in my barrier to let it embrace me as he wrapped a hand around my waist and pulled me in for a kiss. Reluctantly I pulled away before we snuck into my car. "We're gonna miss the signing."

Tucker sighed and slowly opened his eyes. "I'd better get in there and make sure the rugrats aren't bothering their mom. Reese doesn't normally mix business with family time. She's really nervous about it."

"Is she?" Odd. I hadn't sensed anything overt. Reese must have it under control, and I had my abilities under control. It really was a new life I was building. It was time to let Tucker in and hope he didn't flee.

We walked in to the browning-sugar smell of chocolate chip cookies in the oven and a gaggle of people crowded into the modest living room. For any crevice that might have been left, joy permeated. It was intense and intoxicating.

Reese had found a seat in a leather armchair, and she pulled out paperwork to set on the coffee table. Since Flores had solved the murder of the psychiatrist and helped get the charges against

her client dropped, Reese agreed to help with the legal paperwork for Emblyn and Emmett.

Austin came in and stepped aside as the newly arrived children rushed through the sliding glass door to the outside. Tucker
squeezed my hand and followed them. As Austin closed the
doors to keep some air conditioning inside, I watched Tucker
shake hands with Tori. He was always so confident and sure of
himself. He'd handle the news of my abilities naturally. He had
to; I wouldn't survive any other way.

Finding a small space beside Hawke—maybe I could lose a
bit of that closet full of guilt by using his real name—I winked at
Emblyn and Emmett, who kept looking out the window at the
children playing in the backyard. Bored maybe, but they didn't
seem nervous at all. Plus, for the first time, I didn't sense an
underlying level of fear. It was good to see them already feeling
at home. Amelia, Gina, and Gina's boyfriend, Daryl, stood closer
to the kitchen. This was what family looked like. We'd be
complete once Forrest and Heidi returned.

Reese offered a pen to Flores as Austin plopped down on the
couch beside him and squeezed his knee. "You know this is just
to finalize the foster arrangement, right? You might need a
bigger house for all the witnesses if the adoption goes through."

Austin grabbed his chest as if in shock. "If? Emblyn and
Emmett are ours."

Flores admonished Austin, but his happiness underneath it
all shown through any cynical statement. "The aunt hasn't been
found, but we have to go through all the proper channels so this
can't be rescinded later." He pulled the Ems' attention with his
serious stare. "But no matter what happens, I personally will
make sure you are safe."

To lighten the mood again, Hawke spoke up. "Hey, now, I'm
on Austin's side here. No *ifs*. The carpool for school has been
set. No takebacksies."

Every time I wondered if I was making a mistake, Austin and
Flores proved they were the right choice. What would I do with

two elementary-aged children anyway? The men knew what Emblyn and Emmett could do and here they could still go to the same school. From what they'd told us, it would be the longest in one place they'd ever been. Plus, I wouldn't be far away to help them with anything Austin and Flores might not be able to tackle.

Flores and Austin took turns initialing or signing wherever Reese pointed for each subsequent piece of paper. The whole thing reminded me of buying a house, and I wasn't sure how comfortable I was with that analogy. Luckily, they'd already been cleared as a foster home, so the paperwork was easy for Reese to push through.

Reese tucked the disheveled pile of papers into a neat stack and offered her hand to the new foster parents. "Congratulations and good luck!"

The room exploded in cheers. The overjoyed emotions filled me like a drug even with my barriers at full charge. Was that what family was supposed to feel like? I could get used to this.

A timer beeping had Austin on his feet. "Okay, everyone, outside! I need room to get to the oven."

The children didn't need to be told twice and would have busted right through the sliding doors if Amelia hadn't quickly opened them.

As we moved outside, Gina leaned over my shoulder, her touch of worry twitched my eye. "Are you sure? I've seen the way those kids look at you."

She was very sweet, but those kids would never be safe with me. And they'd been through enough. To Gina, I replied, "I live in a one-bedroom townhouse. Where would I put them?"

"Yea," Amelia agreed from my other side. "Plus, she'd have to hide all of that alcohol. They'll be teenagers in two shakes."

"Ha, ha, ha," I said, though she wasn't wrong about the amount of liquor I kept in the house. But that was a problem for another day.

Daryl held up three solo cups. "Did I hear a request for alcohol? I retrieved these from the boldly labeled *adult beverage container*. I'm assuming that means it's liquored up."

"That's exactly what it means." Amelia gladly took one from him, then turned to Gina. "He's handy. You can bring him around more."

She smiled at her new beau and took a cup. "I think I just might."

The flustered joy of Daryl tickled my fingers. When he offered me the last cup, I shook my head. "You keep it. I need to rescue Tucker from uncle duty."

The three toasted and chatted as I walked off. It didn't take long to free Tucker from the gaggle of children who begged him to push three at a time on the swing set. "Sorry, guys, I need Uncle Tuck for a little bit."

Amidst the groans of disappointment, Tucker promised them he'd be back later. We made our way to the side of the house to a manicured garden and a cushioned bench. As we took our seat, the way he looked at me made all the parts that weren't touched by the sun heat up and tingle. Without saying a thing, I leaned up and he leaned down. When our lips touched, the warmth in my lustful parts spread to my entire body until my barrier shook with the intensity of it all.

Before I gave in and drug him off to the guest room, I pulled away. "I'll never get tired of that."

The way Tucker smiled at me was enough for me to believe in true love. "I'll make sure you don't."

An ache bubbled behind my heart as fear at what was to come next almost made me run away instead. But not this time. "Tucker, remember what I said about Heidi being able to heal with some sort of supernatural ability?"

Tucker sat back against the bench, but still angled toward me. "It's not something one forgets."

Okay, don't panic yet. Keep going. "Well, she's not the only one."

My eye twitched as Tucker's anxiety grew, but in that suppressed memory kind of way. "Go on."

I puffed out a deep breath and steadied myself. "It's probably best if I showed you." Whelp, it was now or never. With my hand held up between us, I closed my fist. All of my anxiety and fear and anger stemming from the fact that I was forced to take this risk just because of who I was pooled under my closed fingers. I snapped them open and on my palm danced a little spark of flame.

Tucker's eyes grew so wide they dominated his face. But instead of running away, he leaned closer. "Cool. What else can you do?"

My relief at his fascination instead of his disgust took over everything else I was feeling and the fire winked out. I jumped on his lap, grabbed his head in my hands, and kissed him over and over again.

Tucker laughed and pulled me closer, intensifying the kiss until I almost couldn't breathe. "Well, I already knew you could do that."

Afraid to ask but needing to hear it, I said, "Are you sure you're okay?"

The man of my dreams held my gaze as if he had some magic of his own. "I don't know if I'm okay with any of this. But I do know that I love you. And I'm willing to go on this journey with you. But there is one thing you have to promise me."

What else could I do but answer, "Anything."

"You can't keep these things from me anymore. If we're going to make a go of this, we have to share the scary things as well as the easy things."

"Deal." Unable to stop myself, I kissed him again.

From around the corner, Amelia whistled at us. "Hey, you two lovebirds. I'm tired of being a third wheel with Gina and Daryl. Come join the party so I can be a fifth wheel."

"We'll be right there." Still holding me in his arms, Tucker stood up from the bench.

Though far from a damsel in distress, there was something so hot about a man lifting me up like that. "I mean, we don't *have* to go back to the party."

He sighed and set me on my feet. "We can continue this later."

I added, "At my place."

As he led me back to the party, he squeezed my hand. "At your place."

I had no idea what Bertram had in store for me or my family, but I was old enough to know you had to enjoy the good moments. I might not be in the middle of happily ever after, but it was certainly a glorious highpoint I planned to hold onto for as long as I could.

A FREE STORY FROM KELLY LYNN COLBY'S BRAIN

Join Kelly's newsletter and keep up with all of her adventurers. She can't wait to take you along for the ride. With a new YA fantasy in progress, an alternative history in the research phase, book four in her paranormal series in the writing stage, and a new short story or two waiting to jump out at her unsuspecting brain, there's always something exciting going on.

Acknowledgments

I have so many people to thank it's daunting. Writing isn't a solitary craft. Well, maybe the actual putting words to screen can be, however, most of us use some sort of accountability/buddy system to help motivate us when everything feels too hard. I'm. Lucky enough to have a healthy supply of help in that area.

To Jean Kenney for giving me the ins and outs of the foster care system in Texas. Thank you for having dinner with me and giving me a clue on how it all works.

To Jess, JoAnna, and Taylor, thank you for our Saturday morning therapy sessions. Talking about our life, day job, writing career, and everything in between over pancakes, eggs benedict, and mushroom flatbread keeps me focused and prevents me from feeling alone. I'm not sure how I survived without our weekly get-togethers.

To a multitude of Twitch streamers who jump on at odd hours just to get some words in, I thank you. Sometimes, I'm like a toddler and I need someone sitting beside me so I keep writing, but I don't want to put pants on. Twitch has solved that problem. I'm sure I'll forget someone, but the ones who have been there for me the most are dhdunn, CoffeeQuills, Raben-Writes, and thewritingtribe. It's so nice to chat for a minute, then write for a sprint, then chat for a minute, then sprint. It might seem slower than simply typing and not stopping until the piece is done. But this is how I progress and y'all get me.

To the accountability group on Cursed Dragon Ship's Discord channel, thank you for sharing your triumphs and struggles and for always being encouraging. I find some groups are positive to a fault. Though optimism has its plac—and I certainly err on the side of being positive—if that's all that's ever shared, then anytime you stumble, the guilt falls down like rain. I mean, no one else is having problems, right? And everyone writes at different speeds. So when only one kind of method is smiled upon, anyone outside those parameters feels left out and inadequate. The writers in the CDS Discord aren't like that at all. Our strength is in supporting each other regardless of the method used to get to the end goal. It's refreshing and I'm a better writer because of it.

To my ever-supportive husband, nothing I do would be possible without Kevin Colby. He works hard to pay the bills so I can pour all of my energy into writing and publishing. Every time I come up with the next crazy scheme, Kevin jumps on board almost more excited than I am. He's a wonderful husband, loving father, and hard worker. I don't know where I'd be without him, but you'd certainly not be holding this book right now. So you should thank him too, because it was good, right?

To the readers, there's no point to any of this without the fans to appreciate the characters and worlds and adventures within the pages. Thank you for taking a chance on a tiny press and its talented authors. As long as you keep reading, I'll keep creating for you. There's no end to the adventures we can go on together.

About the Author

Kelly Lynn Colby has tried to write mundane stories but magic always sneaks its way in. The result? The YA epic fantasy duology The Recharging (complete) and the paranormal thriller series Emergence (book three in 2023). The first is safe for young readers while the second is better for adult eyes. She's learned a ton from her short stories as well which you can find in a plethora of anthologies. When she's not traveling the country attending publishing or pop culture conventions, Kelly writes fiction and answers an inordinate number of emails at her cluttered desk, coffee shops, and parks in Houston, Texas.

facebook.com/kcolbywrites
twitter.com/kcolbywrites
instagram.com/kcolbywrites

Also by Kelly Lynn Colby

Missed Book One? Check out *The Collector* and see how Fauna's journey began.

A curse can be a gift until it makes you the target of a sadistic killer.

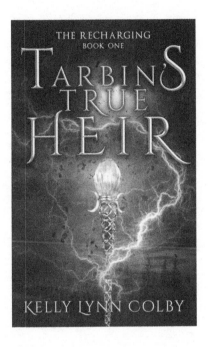

When magic is rediscovered in a land devoid of it, the royal twins must compete to earn the right to be called True Heir, a title that means more than either imagined.

Made in the USA
Monee, IL
10 November 2023